The Battle for Skillern Tract

When desperate ex-Confederate officer Zac Hunter rides into Nacogdoches, he has his mind set on bank robbery. What he finds when he walks into the bank is a robbery already in progress and town marshal Dan McCrae dying from gunshot wounds.

Hunter is accused of murder by Councillor Morgan Jarrow, then abruptly offered the job of town marshal. He is forced to serve notice on businessmen drilling for oil on the Skillern Tract, crosses swords with lawyer Tyne Coburn and the two gunslingers Yantze and Levin, and must decide if Deputy Quint's strange confession is the truth.

As the various factions in Nacogdoches struggle for supremacy, Hunter is drawn into a vicious cycle of treachery and murder. The showdown would come in a blazing gunfight on the Skillern Tract.

www.johnpaxtonsheriff.co.uk

The Battle for Skillern Tract

MATT LAIDLAW

A Black Horse Western

ROBERT HALE · LONDON

© Matt Laidlaw 2009
First published in Great Britain 2009

ISBN 978-0-7090-8800-4

Robert Hale Limited
Clerkenwell House
Clerkenwell Green
London EC1R 0HT

www.halebooks.com

Typeset by
Derek Doyle & Associates, Shaw Heath
Printed and bound in Great Britain by
CPI Antony Rowe, Chippenham and Eastbourne

PART ONE

ONE

10 September, 1866

Hunter broke camp in the luminous half light that comes a long time before true dawn. He kicked earth over the embers of his breakfast fire, then rode out of the cottonwoods and forded the ox-bow on the Sabine River. Slick wet stones clattered under the iron of his horse's shoes. The morning river mist swirled around the big blood bay's hocks. With soft words and a sharp flick of the reins Hunter urged the reluctant horse through the water, up the far bank and onto Texas soil. By sunrise he had put the Sabine ten miles behind him; by the time the sun's heat beating on the back of his neck was uncomfortable he had covered the full thirty miles to Nacogdoches and was able to look down over the sprawling town from a low rise.

A hot wind had picked up and he could taste the East Texas dust like grit on his teeth as he dismounted. His mount had turned its tail to the wind and was standing patiently, head down, legs braced. Steadying himself by leaning back against the saddle, Hunter looked across the dark timber cloaking the undulating terrain for as far as the eye could see, then down towards the clearing on the muddy river. Then, lifting to his eyes the French field-glasses he'd carried with him through The War between The States, he studied the layout of Nacogdoches' rutted streets. He adjusted the knurled focusing wheel and used the strong magnification to pull residential properties, commercial premises, horses and riders and people on foot so close he could have been studying them from across the street.

Activity, but not too much. Few people about that early in the morning, and from where he was, almost a mile away, Hunter had the benefit of one-way observation: he could look without being seen, and what he was looking for was the town's bank. Quickly finding the ugly building standing on one side of the town's wide square, his belly was gripped by a nervous cramp and suddenly his mouth was so dry he couldn't spit. Through the glasses he was having difficulty holding steady he could see that the bank's doors were open for business. The hitch rail in front of the building was empty. He doubted if the morning's first customers had arrived. There was nothing stopping him from riding down there, walking in through those doors with a drawn gun and, for the first time in his life, committing armed robbery.

6

And walking out again, less than five minutes later, a rich man. Maybe. If the cashier played ball. If there was no guard armed with a shotgun. If the manager cared more for his wife and family than he did for the bank's money. A lot of ifs. Too many of them. But what the hell kind of choice did he have?

The wind hissed through the trees as he stowed the glasses in his saddle-bag, finding himself fumbling like a frightened school kid with strap and buckle. Parched leaves rustled overhead like dry paper, and the big horse whickered softly. Hunter pulled his threadbare Confederate army jacket about him as if to cocoon himself against the rising fear that was causing his thigh muscles to tremble. With cold deliberation he fought that fear by slipping from its holster his converted 1861 Colt Navy revolver, pulling the hammer back to half-cock and opening the loading gate to the side then spinning the cylinder with his thumb so that the bases of the five rim-fire cartridges glittered in the sun.

He grunted with satisfaction. Enough gleaming metal in that weapon, even without pulling the trigger, to scare the hell out of ordinary bank tellers or a manager conscious of his own thin hide. He snapped shut the gate and holstered the .38, then reality forced him to revise that opinion: the finest weapon in the West would be of no use to him if the manager turned out to be a hero with a scattergun under the counter and Hunter had to fight his way out. Blasting his way out of the bank would put him out on the street. On the street, a lonely figure in that wide square, he'd be as exposed as a beetle on a white bed-sheet. And it wasn't the ordinary citizens of

7

Nacogdoches who were cause for concern.

A final sweep of the field-glasses before he'd lowered them had told Hunter that the town marshal's office and jail lay almost directly across the square from the bank. The rattle of gunfire emerging from the town's financial centre would surely bring the marshal and his deputies tumbling out onto the street and leave Hunter stranded and looking at a long spell in the Texas state penitentiary, or a sudden, violent death.

So it was a toss up, Hunter thought bitterly. Turn back to the Sabine, or ride into the town, rob the bank, and ride out with a gunny-sack stuffed with cash.

His choice. The first option was the safe one; the second could see his bloody body sprawled in the dust of that square, used bank-notes spilling from the fallen gunny-sack to be caught and whirled aloft by the wind.

Not an easy decision to make, but not too difficult either if the man looking at those choices was alone in the world. The complication here was that if Hunter took the second option, and died in the attempt, the real loser would be a hard-working, lonely widow. Twenty-four hours ago, Alice Hunter had watched her only son ride away from their Louisiana homestead at Natchitoches on the Cane River. No word of where he was heading. No suggestion of when he'd be back. What he had told her, with as much conviction as he could muster, was that when he did return their troubles would be over. Money would no longer be a problem and she would be able to give up her work in the town's one greasy café.

Well, Hunter thought, in a short while he'd be making all her dreams come true, or eating his words in what would certainly be his own last supper. Because there was no decision to be made. That had been made seven days ago when he rode home from the war to find his pa long dead, his ma living in poverty and his own prospects as bleak as a New York blizzard.

TWO

The town of Nacogdoches was a settlement of mostly run-down shacks and two storey business premises with flimsy false fronts clustered on both sides of a slow-running creek that was an unnamed minor tributary of the Sabine, which itself was formed by the confluence of the Cowleech Fork, Caddo Fork, and South Fork rivers. Hunter's field-glasses had not lied. Some shops and businesses were open as he rode in – pale skirts swirled in the shadowy gloom of the general store; a cowpoke was walking his horse in through the wide doors of the livery barn; an old man with long grey hair was standing gazing up at the swirls of red and white on the pole outside the barber's shop – but the square when he reached it was hot, dusty and deserted. Almost. In the time it had taken for him to ride in from his observation point atop that low rise, two riders had hitched their horses to the peeled-pine rail in front of the bank.

A quick glance across the square at the marshal's office revealed no movement, no sign of life. He'd be at breakfast, Hunter reckoned, either in his office or eating fried steak and eggs washed down with black coffee in the town's café. The marshal, and maybe one deputy. If there was a second, he'd be the night man. That put him at home, in bed, snoring, but the others too damn close for comfort. The square, as he'd observed from afar, was a potential death-trap.

Jaw tense, Hunter swung down in front of the bank. He loose-tied the bay alongside the two ragged broncs standing hip-shot in the hot sun, took a folded gunny-sack out of his saddle-bag and tucked it into his gun-belt. Then he stood for a moment, as if deep in thought, hoping to give the appearance of a businessman getting clear in his mind the financial transactions that lay just moments ahead. That brought a thin, humourless smile to Hunter's lips. Some businessman, he thought, and the legality of the so-called transaction he had in mind was surely open to question.

Strangely, the proximity to his goal had steadied his nerves. He'd thought about pulling up his bandanna as a crude mask, but realization that if this one-man raid on the Nacogdoches bank was a success he'd be splashing back through the Sabine river and into Louisiana before nightfall made him reject the idea. Besides, he'd figured, who in his right mind recalls with any accuracy the face of a man holding a cocked pistol to his belly?

A broad stone step led up to the bank's doors. Hunter tilted his head, heard the sound of men talking with raised voices inside the building and looked back briefly but with a spark of renewed interest at the two broncs tethered alongside the bay. Then, deliberately concentrating solely on the task that lay ahead, he

11

stepped up and began to push open the heavy doors.

At once his ears were assailed by a thunderous fusillade of gunfire. Stunned, his ears ringing from the roar of exploding shells, he counted six or more shots in the furious volley. Then the firing ceased. Caught by indecision, his mind a whirl of confusion, Hunter realized instinct had made him draw his six-gun. That settled it; he was halfway there. Gritting his teeth, he pushed the door all the way open. Then he sprang inside the bank, stepped to one side and flattened himself against the wall.

The air stank of cordite. Gunsmoke was a blue haze drifting towards the overhead oil lamps. Two men stood in the centre of the small room. Their menacing presence made them loom large. The small room seemed overcrowded. They were between Hunter and the cashiers' counter. They held empty gunny-sacks and smoking six-guns. A third man was slumped against the side wall. Wide of shoulder, heavy of frame, he was slowly sliding down the wall as if the strength was leaking from his legs. A shield glittered on his vest. His shirt was blood-soaked, his moustachioed face a red mask. His staring grey eyes were filmed by death.

In the fraction of a second it took for Hunter to take in the scene, a cool draught swept through the room and caught the door. It swung on oiled hinges, then slammed shut with a bang. The two men caught in the centre of the room whirled to face Hunter, boot-heels squeaking on the board floor. Long-barrelled pistols lifted. Unshaven faces twisted in shocked snarls. The gunmen's hair was lank and greasy. Above the stink of cordite

Hunter caught the reek of horse sweat from their stained pants.

Their eyes narrowed. Hunter registered that instant of decision, knew their fingers were tightening on triggers; knew that in the next fraction of a second he could die, or fight to stay alive.

He sprang sideways. His Colt came up and level. He dropped to a half-crouch and snapped off two rapid shots. Both bullets slammed into living flesh. The two men staggered backwards. Six-guns fell from suddenly nerveless hands, clattering on the boards. Again Hunter cocked the big Colt with his thumb. Then he saw that no third shot was necessary. Both men fell heavily to the floor. Their bodies were borne down by the weight of the angel of death settling on their shoulders. They lay unmoving. The sudden quiet in the bank was the silence of a chapel when the last throat has been cleared before the final hymn.

Then the door was kicked open.

Three men tumbled over the threshold. The first man in was long and lean, wore a badge on his vest and carried a six-gun as if it was something strange he'd picked up in the street. He was followed by two men in dark suits powdered with dust. One was small, with pale blue eyes and thin grey hair almost covering a pink scalp.

The other was big, and dangerous. He walked in last. His penetrating eyes, unblinking as a rattlesnake's, weren't missing a trick.

In a flash, Hunter saw the situation through the eyes of the newcomers. He was the only man standing inside the bank. The air was acrid with gunsmoke. He was holding a pistol that had been fired. Three men lay dead or dying on the floor. One of those men was a lawman. His shirt was blood soaked. He was an ageing lawman: his hat had fallen off exposing grizzled grey hair, and his shirt was soaked in blood.

'What the hell kept you so long?' Hunter said to the man he guessed was a deputy, grabbing the initiative and using it in the hope of knocking the more dangerous big man off his stride. 'If I hadn't walked in when I did—'

'Drop that pistol, now,' the big man said. And he lifted the Greener shotgun he'd been holding unseen alongside his right leg and levelled it at Hunter. 'Drop it, or I drop you – and believe me, there's nothing I'd enjoy more.'

For a long moment, Hunter hesitated. The three new arrivals were between him and the door. Out of the corner of his eye he detected movement, and knew that terrified bank employees were emerging from hiding places. One would be the manager, or owner. His courage would be returning. Humiliation would be replaced by anger. And there'd be a gun of some kind behind the counter, effectively stopping any hope of escape in that direction.

Then, as if he'd soaked up some of the big man's power, the skinny deputy with the high cheekbones of an Indian stepped forward. He grabbed a handful of shirt and rammed his pistol up under Hunter's chin.

'Do as Jarrow says.'

Head back, Hunter drew a deep breath, expelled it, then let his Colt slip from his fingers.

As it hit the floor, the big man stepped forward. He

pushed the deputy aside and kicked Hunter's Colt across the room. Then he took a half step back to give himself space, swung the shotgun by its stock and slammed the double barrels against Hunter's jaw.

Pain knifed through Hunter's face, flashed like liquid fire behind his eyes. He lurched backwards, cracking his head hard against the wall. Coppery liquid pooled in his mouth. He shook his head, spat out a fragment of broken tooth, felt blood dribble down his chin. Carefully, he wiped it away with the back of his hand, never taking his eyes off the man with the shotgun.

The third man, the small fellow with pale-blue eyes, stepped forward with his mouth open as if to protest. Jarrow waved him away.

'That was to put you in the right mood,' he informed Hunter pleasantly.

'It had the wrong effect,' Hunter said. 'All it's done is made me remember your face.'

'Dead men don't have memories,' Jarrow said. 'You'll hang for murder.'

'I saved your town's cash. Shot dead two bank robbers.'

'That's not what I see,' Jarrow said. 'How about you, Quint?' He looked at the rawboned deputy. 'How d'you read this situation?'

'Those two' – the deputy pointed at the two dead men – 'planned on robbing the bank, but walked straight into a heap of trouble. Marshal McCrae was already in here. I know Dan McCrae's capabilities with a gun: they stood no chance, and he downed them easy. Then their pard walked in, and I guess McCrae wasn't expecting a third man 'cause he took this third fellow's slugs in the head and chest.'

'Strachan?' Jarrow look questioningly at the little man, who had now backed away.

That worthy cleared his throat, then shrugged uncertainly. 'I suppose that's one possible interpretation of events—'

'The only one,' Jarrow cut in with a growl.

Hunter shook his head. 'Look at them.' He swung an arm, gesturing at the board floor, the bodies of the filthy, unshaven men he'd shot. 'Do I look like them, do I look like a bank robber?'

'To me, you look like a cool, efficient killer,' Jarrow said. 'A ringleader. Those two fools were seen entering the bank. Then we heard gunshots. Seconds after those gunshots, you followed them in and we heard two more shots as we ran across the square. We burst in here, McCrae's taken two slugs and you're standing holding that smoking pistol.' He gestured over his shoulder at Hunter's Colt. 'You denyin' any part of that?'

'No. Why should I? That's exactly the way it happened.'

'Right. McCrae shot your partners, you walked in and put two shots into McCrae.'

'Wrong—'

'You followed them in—'

'Yes. But that doesn't make me one of them.'

'That does,' Jarrow said, and he pointed at the gunny-sack tucked in Hunter's gun-belt.

In the sudden silence a man in white shirt, string tie and dark trousers appeared on the other side of the

16

counter, lifted a flap and came through. The shirt was stained with sweat under the arms. His plump face was pale and glistening. He wore spectacles, and his soft hand shook as he lifted it to adjust them.

Jarrow swung towards him.

'What happened here, Soames?'

'I opened up, as always, first man in was Marshal McCrae.'

'What about Wilson, is he here?'

'Mr Wilson,' Soames said prissily, 'never gets here before ten, as is his privilege as the bank's manager.'

'OK, so there's you and McCrae. What happened next?'

'Then those two men walked in.' Soames looked down at the two dead men, and shuddered. 'I saw their pistols and guessed what was about to happen. To protect the bank's assets, I remained behind the counter and took cover.'

'I'll bet you did,' the lean deputy, Quint, said, grinning. 'So what it amounts to is you saw nothing?'

'I saw enough.'

'Not nearly enough for our friend here,' Quint said, and he looked at Jarrow as if awaiting orders.

He's either out of his depth because suddenly he's acting town marshal, Hunter thought, or there's hidden currents here and he's waiting to see which way they flow, and how fast. But what does that make Jarrow? He admits he saw two gunmen enter the bank. That means he and Quint were watching what they must have known was a bank robbery about to happen. If they were watching, what took them so long to get over here? Were they

17

expecting McCrae to make short work of those fellows – or the exact opposite? The only certainty is they took their time crossing that square. So if they're not naturally slow moving, and they didn't make a serious miscalculation, then there's something going on here in Nacogdoches that stinks worse then a dead skunk.

'There's some tidying up to do,' Jarrow said, cutting through those disturbing thoughts. 'Soames, you wait here until your boss arrives. Strachan, on the way back to your office get Sam Allman over here with his buckboard to cart these bodies away.'

Then he fixed his gaze on Hunter.

'What did you say your name was?'

'Hunter. Zac Hunter.'

'Well, Zac Hunter, you can unbuckle that gun-belt, then you're coming across the street with me and Quint. There's a clean, empty cell waiting for you, and in a short while there'll be a fellow along with a length of hemp he'll use to measure your neck for the hangman's noose.'

THREE

They left him alone with the early morning sun slanting through the high barred window of the cell painting broad stripes across his chest as he lay on the cornhusk mattress with his hands clasped behind his head. As time passed by he heard the rattle of the buckboard the man Jarrow had called Strachan had summoned, listened to the voices from across the square and three faint but clearly heavy thumps as dead bodies were loaded onto the wagon. More rattling, the jingle of harness, the stamp of hoofs moving away from the square as the buckboard transported the dead men away and into the care of Nacogdoches' undertaker. And, gradually, as the sun rose higher and the town came to life, Hunter allowed the buzz of normalcy to settle around him like a shield and slipped into a troubled doze.

He came awake in the hot cell to a sweat-dampened face and a dry mouth. As he touched his tender jaw with his fingers and used his tongue to probe the tooth chipped by the blow from the shotgun barrel, he was experiencing the same sense of isolation that had gripped him like the chill of a northern winter and remained with him ever since the cell door clanged shut and the key turned in the lock. And yet, he thought, there's still hope. The angle of the sun's rays told him that he had slept for a couple of hours. Undisturbed. No man with work-roughened hands and a rope to measure his neck. No lynch mob hammering at the doors and baying for his blood.

Hunter smiled at those thoughts for, with his mind refreshed by sleep, he was convinced that his assessment of the situation in the bank had been entirely accurate: instinct was telling him that something in that room had been badly wrong. But it was a cold smile. The dark thoughts that had arrived unbidden and refused to go away were telling him that, if asked to put a finger on it, he would say that what he'd stumbled on was not a bank robbery, but an arranged, cold-blooded murder.

'Well now, why the hell am I not surprised?' Hunter said when, some fifteen minutes later, the key was turned in the lock, the door swung open and the man called Jarrow walked into the cell.

'You tell me,' Jarrow said, settling his bulk comfortably at the foot of the iron cot and leaning back against the stone wall.

'Because it was obvious from the demeanour of those men in the bank that they're bit players,' Hunter said. 'A deputy was there, but he looked like an actor in the wrong role, holding the wrong prop.'

'The six-gun?' Jarrow shrugged. 'Quint's out there now, in the office. You try to make a break, you'll discover that he's a fine shot.'

'If he's got that skill, he got it shooting ducks, not outlaws.'

'And from the look of that jacket you got yours shooting Yankee soldiers out of the saddle.'

'Which strikes me as highly irrelevant. If dead men don't have memories, they sure as hell can't squeeze a trigger.'

'Is that what I said?' Jarrow looked amused.

'You also told me a man would be visiting me with a length of hemp for my neck. That hasn't happened.'

'There's still time.'

'Yeah,' Hunter said, 'but for what? What the hell's going on, Jarrow?'

The big man grinned, but his eyes were thoughtful.

'That might be the wrong tone of voice to use, feller. If I was here to get you out of trouble, it could make me change my mind.'

'A man who's done no wrong,' Hunter said, 'doesn't need extricating.'

'Big word. The problem is, what went on in the bank this morning wasn't witnessed. Three men died in there, one walked out with a weak story to tell. Seems to me I'm free to put my own interpretation on events.'

'To further your own ends?'

'How about yours and mine? Seems to me they coincide.'

'Now there's a concept that stretches the imagination.'

'No. It's your neck that's going to be stretched for the cold-blooded murder of the town's marshal.'

'This is getting tiresome,' Hunter said. 'I told you: when I walked into the bank, McCrae was already dead or dying. He'd been shot by one or both of those outlaws.'

'Circumstantial evidence suggests otherwise,' Jarrow said. 'But either way, McCrae's death leaves Nacogdoches without a marshal.'

'Promote Quint.'

Jarrow laughed. 'You've already expressed your opinion of our esteemed deputy. I tend to agree. However, looking on the action in the bank from a different viewpoint, it's not too difficult to find a more suitable man for the job.'

For a few moments there was quiet in the cell. Jarrow was relaxed, at ease with himself, as he waited for a reaction. Hunter was unable to wipe the frown from his face as he chewed over what he'd heard.

In the bank he had sensed that there were undercurrents of tension which had nothing to do with the violence that left three men dead. Indeed, if he looked back on what had happened, the action was a straightforward gunfight. Bank robbers had been caught cold by a courageous town marshal. The marshal had been shot dead. Then Hunter walked in, and had bested the two gunmen and left them dead on the floor.

The real tension, as opposed to the natural rush of adrenaline caused by involvement in violent action, had been noticeable from the moment Jarrow burst into the bank. His presence was powerful, his intentions unclear and therefore disturbing and creating uneasiness in all those at the scene. The tension directly attributable to his presence had increased when the unfolding story made it clear that Jarrow and the useless town deputy had watched from across the square as the two gunmen walked into the bank, but had held back and done nothing.

If they'd watched the gunmen walk into the bank, it was logical to assume that they'd also seen Marshal McCrae. According to Soames, the bank's teller, the lawman was first man in; as the bank had just opened, he could have been only minutes ahead of the two bank robbers. And, despite his obvious incompetence, even from a distance Deputy Quint must have realized what was about to happen and understood that it was his duty to help the marshal. Yet he too had held back. Why?

'What the hell are you, Jarrow?' Hunter said softly.

'Leader of the town council. Mayor. A man aiming to be very rich, in a very short time.' The big man shrugged, as if dismissing the idea as inconsequential, but the hard look in his eyes belied those sentiments and, not for the first time, Hunter wondered just what kind of an unlawful conspiracy he'd stumbled into.

'Did getting rich quick require the elimination of the town marshal? Did he have relatives? A wife, children – a brother?'

Jarrow said nothing. The hard look remained. A muscle twitching in his jaw was the only sign of emotion.

'Were those bank robbers in your employ?' Hunter went on. 'If you sent them in to murder McCrae, and he does have a brother, you could be in trouble. Or was my arrival a stroke of luck, my fast gun eliminating dangerous witnesses and so wrapping everything up in a tidy package you could dump in a trash can?'

'I need an answer,' Jarrow said.

'And I need the question. Spell it out, Jarrow.'

'What's it to be? A rope, or a badge?'

'You say you're the town mayor. That doesn't make you all powerful. The appointment of a new town marshal will require the approval of a majority of councillors.'

'Usually more than that. This is the Nacogdoches county seat. That means there's a sheriff. However, he's out of town for a couple of weeks, called to Washington for some kind of seminar or convention. In his absence, the councillors will do as I say.'

'Is that a fact?' Hunter said thoughtfully.

'It is, and I'll give you another: if you accept the offer and pin on that badge, I'll have a new town marshal forced, by circumstances, into that same position: you'll be in my pocket, Hunter. No question about it. But it's that, or I walk out of here and the next sound you hear will be a carpenter out back hammering nails into the timber of your personal scaffold.'

FOUR

Though he had been tardy in going to the aid of Marshal McCrae, naturally slow moving was not a description that would fit Jarrow. Zac Hunter decided that when he found himself, fifteen minutes later, sitting behind the desk in the office of the late Marshal Dan McCrae with a shiny badge pinned to his Confederate jacket and a pot of coffee bubbling away on the black iron stove.

If Jarrow had got rid of McCrae because the old marshal was opposing some kind of skulduggery Jarrow was involved in, then he had been quick to see the advantage of handing the badge to a man who was handy with a six-gun but living in the shadow of the hangman's noose.

That noose, at first glance, was held or controlled by Jarrow. In fact, Hunter reflected, he might be quick, but the big man certainly wasn't over endowed with brains. By handing him the marshal's badge, Jarrow seemed to be telling the people of Nacogdoches that Hunter had his confidence, and was an innocent man – in a word, letting him off the hook. Also, looked at from another angle, if Hunter had murdered McCrae – and there were no witnesses to the killings in the bank – then by handing over the badge Jarrow had made himself an accessory to murder. Which meant that, guilty or innocent, Hunter was now free to walk away if he chose to do so. Jarrow couldn't stop him. For if Hunter went down, Jarrow would surely go down with him.

Conclusion: the big man had put himself in a precarious situation that hadn't existed before the fiasco at the bank. Also, he now had a stranger in the camp, a man about whom he knew absolutely nothing.

Well, there was a bitter irony in there somewhere, Hunter mused, because after the day's events he was having a hard time recognizing himself. When he crossed the Sabine river in the cold pre-dawn light, he'd been setting out to rob a bank. Instead, he'd gunned down two outlaws and finished up as town marshal.

Hunter thought about that for a moment, mild amusement tempered by a huge chunk of disbelief, then swung out of the swivel chair, poured scalding hot coffee into a tin cup and strolled to the open door.

It was afternoon, and the sun's heat rose in shimmers from the dust. Hunter could smell horses, the dry timber of the buildings, the ranker odour of the nearby sluggish creek. From the doorway he had a clear view across the wide square to the bank. His big bay was still there, but the outlaws' horses had been moved. With everything tidied up – as Jarrow had quaintly put it – the bank was doing its usual business.

As Hunter watched, Quint emerged, stared moodily

26

across at the jail then set off at a diagonal that would take him to Nacogdoches main street. Was the deputy peeved at not getting the top job, Hunter wondered?

Sipping his coffee and gazing across the plank walk, he wondered idly what, as marshal, he was supposed to be doing. A reasonable monthly wage had been mentioned and, as far as Hunter knew, a town marshal was a policemen who undertook mundane tasks such as the collection of fines imposed for minor ordinance offences. Only rarely did he tackle outlaws, and almost always it would be in close consultation with the Nacogdoches county sheriff.

But Jarrow had said very little, given no instructions. He'd accompanied Hunter from the cell, pinned on the badge, shaken the new marshal's hand with a glint of amusement in his dark eyes, then walked out. Heading, Hunter realized, in the same direction as that taken by Quint.

But so what? Nacogdoches had one main street. Any business to be conducted by either man would be in premises located on that street. Hunter had ridden into town from that direction, and he recalled a general store, the livery barn, and . . . and what else? A saloon: The Old Colonial. A gunsmith. A café. A door bearing the brass plate of an attorney at law.

Hunter took another drink, found his mouth filled with coffee grounds, spat and sent the rest of the foul liquid splashing into the dust.

Back at the desk, he sifted idly through the papers: wanted dodgers, advertisements for everything from lye soap and ladies underwear to a forthcoming country fair.

Tucked away, a copy of the local newspaper. Not recent. Hunter checked the date. It was an issue from the previous year, December 1865. And it had been carefully folded so that one article took prominence.

Hunter picked it up, turned his chair so that the sunlight fell on the page, and skimmed though the article. The gist was that a man called Lyne Taliaferro Barret had established the Melrose Petroleum Oil Company and taken out a fresh lease on land at Oil Springs. Some background was given. It seemed that the original lease had been taken out in 1859, Barret had begun drilling for oil, but the war had intervened.

Hunter put down the folded newspaper, rocked gently, thoughtfully.

If Barret had been drilling in 1859, he had the equipment already on the site at Oil Springs. It was now September '66, the new lease had been taken out ten months ago. Allow a month for the legal process and necessary checking of the rig. That suggested at least nine months' drilling. How deep, Hunter wondered, could an oil company drill in that time?

Then Hunter frowned, and narrowed his eyes. The big question, he realized, was not how deep the company could drill, but how deep they needed to drill to find oil. And what any of that had to do with the man called Jarrow admitting that his aim was to get very rich, in a very short time.

He still sitting in warm afternoon sun, ruminating and trying hard to stay awake, when a man with a drooping moustache and wise eyes stamped into the office.

*

'Just look at you,' the newcomer said scathingly and without preamble. 'You rode in to rob a bank, and now you're like a cow finds itself with one horn snagged by a 'puncher's rope.'

'Just one?'

'That's it. I'm not saying you're finished. There's still time to get loose if you do some fast thinking. But from where I stand I can see that 'puncher's got a dally around the horn, he's working his horse hard to keep the rope taut, and I never saw a cow yet that was renowned for its thinking powers.'

'What makes you think I intended to rob the bank, Mr. . . ?'

'Frank Leland,' the man said. 'Town gunsmith. Saw you ride in, that's why. No mistaking that look, even from a distance. Your eyes were unfocused, your mind contemplating actions not in the realm of ordinary mortals.'

'If that's true, why am I sitting here wearing a lawman's badge?'

Leland moved away from the door, swept his Stetson from his head and waved it to indicate the desk.

'If you've been reading that newspaper, you've given yourself part of the answer. Mix Morgan Jarrow into the equation, and you're halfway there.'

'You're talking in riddles, Leland.'

'Any talk here in Nacogdoches,' Leland said, 'is safer when it's done in that fashion.' He looked shrewdly at Hunter. 'I can't see riddles fooling a man like you for too long.'

Hunter rocked gently, studied the lean man who knew

guns and was now sitting with his haunch on a corner of the desk.

'If it's not too risky, would you mind getting to the point?'

Suddenly deadly serious, Leland said, 'I came in here to take a look at you, Hunter, because I consider myself to be a good judge of men. That's done. Now I'm about to give you a friendly warning. You've probably figured out some of what's going on here – if you haven't, you damn soon will – but, if the saying can be applied to a town, remember this: still waters run mighty deep.'

'You saying certain factions are working towards the downfall of Morgan Jarrow?'

Leland's eyes were wide and innocent as he stepped away from the desk and donned his hat.

'Some big words are beyond my understanding,' he said, 'and if I mentioned any names in this office then my memory's seriously failing me.' He grinned and nodded. 'See you around, Marshal.'

'Who the hell is Tyne Coburn?'

'Lawyer,' Quint said. 'Set up office six months ago, about a month before Morgan Jarrow rode into Nacogdoches.'

'And he wants to see me?'

'Nope, *Jarrow* wants you to see him.'

'Isn't that the same thing?'

Quint had walked in ten minutes after Frank Leland walked out, and five minutes after Hunter had given up some puzzled pondering on the gunsmith's motives.

Now Quint said not a word. Instead he simply met

Hunter's level gaze and, in that instant, Hunter revised his opinion of the lean deputy with the face of a hungry Indian. For in those grey eyes, clear for all to see, there was a depth of intelligence that had not been noticeable in their earlier encounters.

'What's Jarrow expect me to do? Introduce myself? Shake the man's hand?'

'Might be an idea, at that,' Quint said, wandering across the office and helping himself to coffee. 'Coburn didn't know you existed until this morning's uproar in the bank.'

'Coburn,' Hunter said. 'The name rings a bell.'

'I wouldn't know,' Quint said. 'I arrived in Nacogdoches about the same time as Jarrow.'

He looked at Hunter over the top of his cup, as if waiting.

'And walked into a job?'

Quint shrugged. 'I walked in here and applied. A more conventional way than the one you adopted. They took me on.'

'They, or Jarrow?'

'The final say was Jarrow's.'

'Not the sheriff's?'

'Town matters are the council's concern.'

'Jarrow arrived in town some five months ago, you say? That would be around May. He arrived in May. And already he's in a position of some power.' Hunter frowned. 'What about the late Marshal McCrae? I'd guess he'd been in office here for many years. Didn't his opinion carry some weight?'

There was something unreadable in Quint's eyes.

31

Once again, he elected to leave the question unanswered.

'OK, so what about this Coburn?' Hunter said impatiently. 'Is he on Jarrow's payroll?'

'Jarrow,' Quint said carefully, 'is leader of the town council. That puts you and me on his payroll. Coburn does some work for them, and gets paid for his services.'

'Doesn't quite answer my question.'

Quint shrugged bony shoulders.

'So, after I've introduced myself to Coburn, what then?'

'I'm just the deputy here,' Quint said softly. 'One of them. There's a regular night man, Scott Tobin, his pa owns the general store.'

'But you know what's going on?'

No answer. Hunter shook his head. Then he came around the desk and grabbed his hat and gun-belt from the peg. He strapped the belt around his waist, settled the Colt on his thigh, slapped on the Stetson and made for the door.

'A word of advice,' Quint said. 'You might find two men sitting in with Coburn. Don't make the mistake of underestimating them. Those two you downed in the bank were fools. Yantze and Levin are an entirely different breed.'

'And on Jarrow's payroll? Like the two in the bank?'

Quint grinned in what looked like approval.

'I'll watch the office: you watch your back.'

FIVE

Hunter hadn't bothered to ask Quint where Coburn's office was located, assuming that the brass plate he'd seen on a door as he rode into Nacogdoches bore the lawyer's name. But before finding out for sure, he had one important chore.

After nodding to Quint and leaving the office he strode across the square. At the hitch rail the hot, tired bay turned its head and greeted him with a soft snort. Hunter patted its damp neck, untied it, then quickly mounted and rode it at a walk across the square and turned into Main Street with its shabby timber buildings and fragile, peeling false fronts. He located the livery barn, rode into the relative cool of the runway. An ancient, bow-legged hostler wearing bib overalls, his bald head covered by a hat from which all colour had been bleached, emerged yawning from a corner office. A silver coin changed hands. The bay was placed in the old man's care.

Back on the street, Hunter quickly discovered that his recollections of the ride into town had been accurate.

The lawyer's office with its gleaming brass plate was a short walk beyond the livery barn and Old Colonial saloon. It was fronted by a wide plank walk. At the hitch rail, three horses were tethered. Hunter remembered Quint's warning.

So, the bold approach, or the timid? He considered his new status, then buffed his badge with his sleeve, tapped on the door and walked in.

Cigar smoke clouded the small room. One man was sitting in a leather chair, his elbows on a solid oak desk, unbuttoned shirt sleeves held back from his wrists by glittering arm bands. His fleshy face was pock-marked. The bloodshot eyes of a drinker glared at Hunter, noted the badge pinned to the Confederate jacket and registered confusion, then swift understanding.

'Do come in, Hunter,' he said, with heavy sarcasm.

Hunter shut the door behind him and cast a glance towards the other two men in the room who were sitting back in worn easy chairs. Tall, raw-boned, and dressed in the nondescript clothing of the range, they were lazily smoking thin cigars. One had long grey hair touching his wide shoulders and a jagged scar on his right cheek that got lost in his drooping moustache. The other man was much younger, with several days' growth of dark beard and slender fingers that were plucking almost incessantly at his whiskers. Both men wore tied-down Colts with walnut butts polished by frequent use. The blankness of their gaze as they returned Hunter's stare was frightening to behold.

'This is our new town marshal,' Coburn went on. 'By all accounts he's a tough fellow. Guns down bank robbers before breakfast. Should have no trouble with Lyne Barret. Hunter, meet Yantze and Levin.'

And meet them with matching force, Hunter decided.

'I know their type,' he said, with scorn in his voice. 'When they're too old to lift a six-gun they do well as clowns in a travelling circus.' He nodded at the grey-haired man. 'He's almost there.'

'That's Yantze,' Coburn said, eyebrows raised. 'I think you've upset him.'

'I'll try not to let it bother me.' Hunter gave the two impassive gunmen a final, contemptuous glance, then turned to the lawyer. 'What do you want from me?'

Coburn sat back, the cigar smouldering between his fingers, his eyes narrowed against the smoke. Behind him the wall was decked with souvenirs: an Indian club, eagle feather hanging limp; an old flintlock holster pistol with engraved barrel.

'You heard me mention Lyne Barret; know anything about him?'

'There's a newspaper in McCrae's office. I read some, and now you're about to tell what it means.'

Yantze spoke for the first time. His voice was soft, but hoarse.

'The man can read,' he said. 'That's always dangerous.'

Levin chuckled. Coburn seemed to be enjoying the atmosphere.

'In this case it's *useful*,' he corrected. 'If you read that newspaper, Hunter, you'll know that last year Barret took out a fresh lease on land thirteen miles or so from here on the Skillern tract. That lease is worthless.'

'Why?'

'The land's sacred. It belongs to the Nacogdoches Indians.'

'That doesn't make sense. Barret's leased the land from Nacogdoches County authorities. If there was a legal objection, based on Indian law or legend, they'd know about it.'

'Maybe they didn't bother to look too hard. After all, Barret's paying good money.'

Hunter grimaced. 'Well, we both know I'm here at the behest of Morgan Jarrow. So I guess he's the man filing the objection, through you. But why should Jarrow object? If Barret strikes oil, he'll bring prosperity to the town. Jarrow heads the town council. He should be backing Barret's endeavours, not trying to bring him down.'

'I work to my client's instructions,' Coburn said. 'The whys and wherefores are not my concern. If an action's legal, I'll see it through.'

'Fair enough. But what part do I play in this?'

'You ride out and talk to Barret.'

'Just Barret. I read something about a Melrose Petroleum Oil Company; a company means more than one man.'

Coburn nodded. 'The others involved are Benjamin Hollingsworth, Charles Hamilton, John Flint, and John Earle.'

'Five men. I'll probably find a couple of them out there, Barret certainly. Do you seriously expect them to up stakes when I give them a tale of Indian mumbo-jumbo?'

'You tell them plainly what you, as an officer of the law, expect them to do.' Coburn shot a glance at Yantze and Levin, then back at Hunter with amusement again flickering in his eyes. 'If they're stubborn, and continue drilling,' he said, 'appropriate action will be taken to ensure they change direction and abide by the law.'

'Your law?' Hunter said. 'Jarrow's law? I can see why you're finding it hard not to laugh: those two clowns sitting over there are closer to the circus than even I imagined. And I've got a sneaking suspicion any action taken by them will be selectively appropriate – meaning it will be heavily biased in favour of your client.'

'My client, your boss,' Coburn said. 'He stepped in when you were in deep trouble, Hunter. But for Morgan Jarrow, you'd be swinging at the end of a rope.'

Hunter grinned. 'Even a shyster like you can see the flaws in that argument,' he said. 'And if you're incensed by those words or my tone,' he went on, as Coburn made as if to rise from his seat, 'take another look at this jacket. I was at Petersburg in '64, under General Beauregard, when a certain lieutenant went missing in the heat of the battle. He was presumed dead. I can see now that was a more than charitable conclusion.'

Quint was coming through from the cells when Hunter got back to the marshal's office. His grey eyes were amused.

'Been making your bed up,' he said. 'This friendly hotel's got rooms to spare, so why walk a hundred yards up the street and pay good money for inferior accommodation?'

'Good thinking,' Hunter said with an answering grin. 'But right now I've got some riding to do. Jarrow has let it be known, through his mouthpiece, that he wants a notice served on Lyne Barret. Coburn said something about the Skillern tract. Thirteen miles or so from here, he said, but in which direction?'

'East. It's wooded country, but you can't miss the tall derrick standing up against the sky.'

Hunter nodded. 'Fair enough. But what's the story on Barret? From reading that newspaper over on the desk I figure drilling began nine months ago. Has he had any luck?'

'You figure wrong. The lease was taken out last December, but drilling didn't start until this summer.'

'And it's now September.' Quint was back at the coffee pot, Hunter watching him and wondering. He said, 'How d'you know so much, Quint? Did you get it all from the newspapers? Or have you been watching the action?'

'I get some details from the paper. It's run by a man called Bart Strachan. Barret comes into town from time to time, and some news of how the drilling's going filters down from the Old Colonial.' Quint shrugged. 'However, he's a businessman hoping to strike oil. That makes him pretty close mouthed.'

'Seems to me,' Hunter said, 'that's a description that could be applied to you.'

'Maybe you don't ask the right questions,' Quint said, abandoning the empty coffee pot and turning to meet Hunter's gaze.

'OK, how about this. Coburn arrives six months ago, he's followed a month later by Jarrow. You arrive around the same time. Am I looking at coincidence?'

'You're looking at facts.'

'All right, then what about Coburn? Was he some kind of an advance party? Put in place to smooth the way for Jarrow?'

'If he did that, I wasn't here to see it.'

'That's right. And when you drifted into town, Jarrow had already taken his place as top man on the town council.'

Hunter walked to the open door and looked out at the late afternoon sunshine. A wagon trundled past, traces jingling, the team kicking up clouds of dust. The square was busy, people going about their business, every one of them casting an eye in Hunter's direction. He narrowed his eyes and averted his head, waited for the dust from the wagon to settle, then gazed thoughtfully across at the bank.

'Whatever's going on here in Nacogdoches, it really started over there, didn't it?' he said without turning. 'Five months after arriving in town and, in my opinion, Jarrow made his first real move. Whatever his plans are, I believe he needed cash, and for some reason he also had to get rid of McCrae without throwing suspicion his way. So he decided to kill two birds with one stone. He hired a couple of outlaws, sent McCrae over to the bank on some pretext just before the time set for the raid. Then I rode in with the intention of robbing a bank, but didn't quite make it. Instead I shot dead the two men who could have been a dangerous liability to Jarrow – but I'm pretty sure I also ruined his plans for getting his hands on the bank's cash.'

A match scratched, and when Hunter turned around he saw that Quint was sitting behind the desk, applying the flame to a cigarette. He smiled ruefully.

'If I hadn't set out to rob a bank,' he said, 'would you be sitting here now wearing that badge?'

'Nope. I'm the ham-fisted fool employed by Jarrow to weaken McCrae's hand. He's got me down for a man who's all thumbs and no brains. I like it that way.'

'Yeah. It allows you to get on with your real job without coming under suspicion. Because I'll bet my last dollar you didn't arrive in Nacogdoches by accident.' He waited, sensed there was no reply coming his way, and said, 'So what is your real job, Quint? Who the hell are you?'

Quint looked as if he was going to let that one slip by. Instead he reached into his vest pocket, took something from it and held the object cupped in his hand as he showed it to Hunter.

'A Texas Ranger,' Hunter said softly, and his eyes widened a little in surprise as he looked at the gold badge with its encircled star. 'Isn't it irregular, or even illegal, for one lawman to hold down a second similar position?' Again no reaction from Quint. He shrugged. 'All right, that tells me your job, but it doesn't explain what a Texas Ranger's doing here in Nacogdoches.'

'No, and for the present that's all you're going to get – and I want what you've just seen kept very quiet indeed,' Quint said, and suddenly the intelligent eyes were cold and hard. 'That's all I've got to say, except for this: just as McCrae was unaware of what he was taking on when he pinned that deputy's badge on my vest, I'll wager Jarrow also made a serious mistake when he took you on the payroll.'

'Does that put us on the same side?' Jarrow said, preparing to leave.

'We'll talk about that,' Quint said, 'if you make it back unscathed from the Skillern tract.'

A casual remark delivered in an offhand manner, Hunter thought dismissively, as he stepped out onto the plank walk, but it was a remark that before too long would come roaring back to haunt him.

SIX

'He's riding out now.'

The small man called Strachan was standing at the window looking down on Main Street. The drum of hoofs could clearly be heard, gradually fading as the rider went on by. Behind him in the room above Coburn's office, Morgan Jarrow was pacing, hands behind his back. He cast a glance towards Coburn, who had come upstairs immediately after the meeting with Hunter.

'Are Yantze and Levin going after him?'

'Just Yantze. He's the better shot. He rode ahead of Hunter. If things seem to be getting too cosy between Hunter and Barret, he'll act.'

'What you mean is, if it looks as if Marshal Hunter's working a double-cross.'

Coburn chuckled. 'What's to double-cross? The man's got a tin badge pinned to his vest, but he's free to ride away. The border's half-a-day's ride away. You were a fool to take him on.'

'Better him than McCrae.'

'Better the devil you know,' Coburn said.

'But not in your case,' Jarrow said with a sneer, 'because Hunter knows you a little *too* well.'

'We're both too well known—'

'For Christ's sake!'

Strachan swore softly as he came away from the window. His face was strained. A nerve was jumping at the corner of one eye.

'This whole thing's madness. You know I've been against it from the start.'

Jarrow's grin was evil. 'You're a councillor, the editor of a small town newspaper. You telling me with honesty that you're against prosperity? Against being rich beyond your wildest dreams?'

'Let Barret get on with it, let him find his oil,' Strachan said, his lips tight. 'The town will still be rich, we'll all benefit in just the same way—'

'But Barret will be in control,' Jarrow cut in.

'Of the oil production. You'll be top man in a boom town. Isn't that enough?'

'There can never be enough,' Jarrow said softly.

There was a bare table in the centre of the room, half-a dozen hard chairs, an oil lamp hanging over the table. Cupboards and bookshelves held papers, files, documents, the typical paraphernalia to be found in the office of any small town's council.

Coburn, sitting at the table, was smoking a cigar and eyeing the little man with displeasure.

'You're either in, or out, Strachan,' he said. 'It was spelt out to you when your council colleagues were dismissed and you were allowed to keep your position.

We sit tight, let Barret do the hard work now. If he strikes oil, we move in. If the site's worthless, we move on.'

Strachan was sweating. 'Move in,' he said. 'Sounds ominous, so what does it mean?'

'We take over the whole operation. Replace Barret and the other members of the Melrose Petroleum Oil Company. Jarrow is elected managing director. The work crew stays on.'

'Barret won't just walk away, and I don't want violence, I won't abide violence.' Strachan shuddered. 'Christ, how I hate all this gunplay.'

Jarrow paused in his pacing. He turned to face the little man, clearly having difficulty hiding his contempt.

'Violence is a last resort, I promise you,' he said, flicking a covert glance towards Coburn. 'We're making a try today. Faced by a lawman questioning his legal right to be there, looking aggressive, giving him what amounts to an ultimatum, Barret may cave in and decide to move on.'

'Rubbish,' Strachan said, almost flinching at his own audacity. 'Barret's got too much of his own money invested. And you, you've got no money. I thought you wanted him to press on, keep drilling, find the oil for you.'

'That's one option. But the operation's up and running. Replacing the men at the top at any time makes no difference to the workers as long as they get their pay at the end of the month.'

But Strachan was already shaking his head in disgust and making for the door. It slammed behind him. There was silence in the room. Then Coburn sighed.

'He's right, you've got no money – and, you know, we should have dumped him with the rest,' he said. 'Sometimes I marvel at the stupid decisions you make.'

'If we surrounded ourselves with fools,' Jarrow said, 'we're unlikely to be threatened by someone inside the tent.'

'You spoke in a similar vein back in '58 when we were going after that operation in Pennsylvania,' Coburn said. 'As I recall, it was someone inside the tent who put the law onto us. Strachan may be mild in appearance, but he's always a danger. Cross him, kick him out on his backside, and he could stop this venture dead with one carefully penned article in that newspaper he runs.'

'Won't happen,' Jarrow said, his jaw tight.

'Make damn sure it doesn't.'

For a moment there was quiet in the room as Jarrow silently fumed. Eventually, he shook his head.

'Moving on, it's obvious this situation's a whole lot different to what went on in '58. This time I've pulled in two experienced gunmen being paid good money to make damn sure we don't fail. Yantze and Levin are the foot soldiers, but with you and me alongside them we've got enough fire power to overcome four businessmen. Also, we both got battle experience with the armed forces' – he grinned wickedly at Coburn – 'even if only one of us served the full term, and on the winning side. Tactically, we'll get it right. With all that going for us, the outcome's not in doubt: if Barret decides to be stubborn, we take them by surprise, hit them hard – and we'll win.'

'He's certainly not going to fall for this Indian legend tomfoolery,' Coburn said sourly. 'I notice you didn't mention that to Strachan.'

'He's been in local government in these parts too long, he'd know it for the nonsense it is.' Jarrow shrugged. 'Anyway, that was your idea.'

'Something I mentioned as a possibility. I never expected you to take it up without consulting me.'

'You aired it, and now I'm using it. If it works – and like Hannum said, there's a sucker born every minute – it'll avert a costly and inevitably very bloody—'

'Oil war?' Coburn suggested.

'Oil war.' Jarrow grinned as he savoured the words. 'You know, Coburn,' he said, 'I'm already beginning to like the sound of that.'

SEVEN

The back room of the Old Colonial, always used by
Cobb, the saloonist, for storage, was standing in as an
office where a private meeting was taking place. There
was a bottle of whiskey standing on a huge crate. Four
glasses, each one almost empty, testified to the nervous
tension permeating the room. Cigarette smoke was a
blue haze thick enough to kill flies. Boxes had been
stacked in front of the only window, blocking out the
afternoon sunshine but also preventing anyone walking
or riding along the back alley from looking in. The oil
lamp standing on one corner of the crate was lit, its
yellow flame wavering only slightly in the stuffy air. The
only ventilation was the imperceptible influx of warm air
through badly-fitting wall-boards for, like the window, the
door was closed. From time to time each of the three
men sitting around the crate glanced anxiously in the
direction of that door, as if at any moment expecting
someone to burst in with a gun.

'It's locked,' Strachan said for the third time, and he held up a key in his fingers, dangling it for them to see. 'Before anyone gets to that door, they have to get past Cobb. You know Cobb, his shotgun and that mean barrel stave he swings, as well as I do: anyone tries to reach us, I reckon the ruckus'll bust our eardrums.'

The three men sitting on smaller boxes arranged around the larger central crate exchanged glances. Strachan was the only man standing – but this was a different Strachan from the man who had burst into the bank, or stormed out of the Nacogdoches council offices. On both of those occasions, and to different onlookers, he had appeared insignificant, a weak man frightened of his own shadow. Now, although he was several inches short of six feet in height, to the men gathered in that back room his stature appeared to be increasing in proportion to his growing air of authority. As he looked at each of the other three men in turn, his pale-blue eyes were flashing dangerously. There was disdain there, too, and perhaps some doubt: here was a man faced with a difficult mission, and he was concerned that the troops at his disposal might not be up to the task.

'I'll ask you again,' he said. 'Do you want your jobs back, do you want to serve on the council of a town that could be rushing towards a time of unprecedented prosperity?'

'And I'll answer those questions,' the town barber, Jake Rogers, said. He was lean, grey, slightly stooped and with a permanent look of uncertainty in his eyes. 'The only man able to give me my job back is Morgan Jarrow.

He won't do that, because he's controlling this town. If Barret strikes oil, Jarrow will control the oil. If the oil brings prosperity, it's Morgan Jarrow who will prosper the most.'

'If Jarrow's no longer in power,' another man said, 'the situation changes. I think that's what Strachan's suggesting.'

The last speaker was the muscular man with a drooping moustache and wise eyes who had only recently come from talking to Zac Hunter. Frank Leland, Nacogdoches' gunsmith, was a respected businessman. His words drew an approving look from Strachan. The newspaper editor had already earmarked Leland, a crack shot, for a leading role in the . . . in what, exactly?

Strachan allowed himself a brief smile at his own moment of uncertainty about his plans – or lack of any. Then he turned his attention to the third man, old Sol Cotter, who ran the town's livery barn. Cotter was wearing his work overalls and the sun-bleached felt hat he undoubtedly slept in. He spent a lot of time sucking mostly toothless gums. From the look in his piercing, sunken grey eyes, he was determined to think hard but say little.

'What about you, Sol?' Strachan said, hoping to draw him out. 'You think it's high time something was done about Jarrow?'

'Have done from the day he dumped every one of us gents but you out on our backsides,' the old man said laconically. 'Trouble is I'm still scratching my head over how to get around them two gunslingers.'

'To scratch your head, Sol,' the gunsmith said, 'you'd need to remove that raggedy item you're using as a hat; to enjoy it, you'd need hair.'

Those comments drew a chuckle from Rogers, but the moment of levity was brief. The old hostler had voiced the obvious objection to a move against Morgan Jarrow. And it was because of the seemingly insurmountable obstacle of two hard-bitten gunmen that Strachan had called the secret meeting.

'Nail on the head, Sol,' he said approvingly. 'The reason no move's been made against Jarrow is because those two mean characters stick close to him, and this is a small town filled with mostly family men reluctant to take risks. I aim to change that.'

'How? Ranchers, 'punchers, people going about their daily lives here in Nacogdoches, they ain't worried about who runs a town so long as it's running smoothly. If what Jarrow's doing works, they'll be happy – and they'll keep their heads down regardless of what you put to them.' The old hostler again, no nonsense, straight to the point. He cocked his bony head, looked keenly at Strachan. 'And why make a move on Jarrow now, when he took over the council and the running of the town way back in May?'

'Should be obvious. Today, in Nacogdoches, an incident occurred in the bank and suddenly everything changed. The old order—'

'New order,' said Leland.

'Yes, I stand corrected, the new order created by Jarrow was knocked sideways, and it was done by one man.'

'The third bank robber, the man who gunned down Marshal McCrae,' Rogers said.

Strachan shook his head. 'I don't believe any of that. I know Jarrow doesn't, though he's keeping his opinion to himself and letting circumstances speak for him. But those circumstances could be misleading and, if I'm right, Hunter walked into a situation where he was faced by two killers, and he downed both of them.

'I strolled in the jail office, had a chat with him,' Leland said. 'He looks straight, to me. When I walked in he'd been reading about Barret and his oil company. He'll put two and two together. While there, I dropped a hint to let him know not everybody in town's browbeaten by Jarrow. His manner suggests he's approachable.

Strachan's face was animated. 'So, are you rating Hunter above McCrae? You raising our hopes, saying he's going to go against Jarrow when McCrae refused point blank?'

'McCrae refused because. . . .' Leland hesitated. 'I think McCrae was looking forward with some yearning towards his retirement, and before he stepped off the fence over Jarrow he wanted to know which way the wind was going to blow.'

'Mixed up way of putting it, but dead right,' Rogers said.

'Yes, and what I'm saying,' Strachan said, 'is we should go talk to Hunter. He's young, he's got no family—'

'That you know of,' Sol Cotter said, sucking his gums.

'Not here, not now,' Strachan said, 'which means they're far enough away to be of no consequence. Also, Jarrow's got him in a stranglehold—'

'Nope,' old Cotter said, 'he's free as a bird, could have rode away soon as that badge was pinned on his vest.'

'But he didn't,' Strachan said softly. 'That has to mean something, so when we go talk to him, that's one of the questions we ask. Why didn't he ride away? Why is he staying in Nacogdoches?'

Rogers had stubbed out his cigarette, and now he drained his whiskey glass and banged it down on the crate.

'There's two of them wearing badges,' he said. 'Have you given a thought to Quint?'

'Quint's a drifter who's struck lucky,' Strachan said. 'I think he's another yes man, a Jarrow man.'

'So any talk with Hunter excludes Quint?'

'Despite my enthusiasm, talk with Hunter will be exploratory.' Strachan's smile was grim. 'That means we're taking nothing at face value. You've already taken a look at this fine upstanding new town marshal, Frank. I liked what I saw of him in the bank – but we need to dig deeper before we take him into our confidence, ask him for help in a venture that could see someone killed. And, yes, it excludes Quint, excludes everybody except the four of us here today. If—'

Old Cotter grinned a toothless grin, and finished the sentence for Strachan.

'If us gents are all in this together,' he said.

'That's it,' Strachan said. 'I intend to bring down Morgan Jarrow. I don't know how. I do know the start must be with Hunter. It's not essential, but I would like the three of you on my side.' His gaze swept the makeshift table. 'A show of hands?'

Two hands were raised. Those of the third man remained palms down on the crate, his fingers touching the empty whiskey glass.

EIGHT

The ride out to the Skillern tract took Zac Hunter slightly to the south of his route into town earlier that day, which explained why, on his way in, he hadn't noticed the oil derrick. Or, he corrected himself, what Lyne Barret hoped would turn out to be an oil derrick. At the moment it was just a timber construction built so that Barret's huge drill could bite its way through earth and solid rock.

The man was living in hope, Hunter figured, which was no bad thing. And at once that thought sent his mind racing back across the Sabine river into Louisiana, where, with agonizing clarity, he could see his mother sitting in her rocking chair on her veranda in the late afternoon sunshine. She was shading her eyes as she gazed yearningly into the crimson skies far to the west, looking for the plume of dust that might signal her son's return. The image brought a lump to Hunter's throat, made him bang his fist on the saddle-horn and reflect with frustration and anger on the way his day had been ruined by circumstances beyond his control.

At which stupidity he did manage a lonely, rueful grin. This day had been ruined, he now realized, not by circumstances, but at the moment back on the home spread when he decided in desperation that robbing a bank was the only way to lift his mother out of poverty. The fact that he'd chosen Nacogdoches as the town to hit was neither here nor there.

He had made a big mistake then, he'd made the mistake potentially fatal by riding to Nacogdoches and stubbornly going ahead with his crazy plan – and still he hadn't learned his lesson; still he couldn't bring himself to make the right, the sensible decision.

He knew Morgan Jarrow had no hold on him once he was out of jail wearing a marshal's badge, yet instead of putting the dust of the town behind him and pointing the big bay towards home, he was doing the bidding of a man he was convinced was evil. Following orders, moreover, passed to him by another man he knew to be an army deserter.

So deep in thought was Hunter that several miles had been covered by his horse at a steady, mile-eating pace before he thought to take stock of his surroundings. When he did, he saw around him thickly wooded, undulating terrain, here and there clearings with glimpses of silver creeks, his own long shadow cast by the lurid rays of the sinking sun lying ahead of him on the rutted trail. A trail over which, he noticed, a haze of fine dust hung as if to jolt him into the realization that along this route a rider had passed. Very recently.

A rider, or riders, Hunter amended. Yantze and Levin. And Hunter cursed softly at his continuing stupidity.

He pulled the horse to the edge of the trail, sat easy in the saddle as he dug out his water bottle and took a quick, cool drink while considering his position.

This development was, he decided, only to be expected. If he knew that Jarrow had but a tenuous hold over him, then a man of Jarrow's calibre would quickly have reached that same conclusion. Sending men after him to monitor the new marshal's behaviour was a natural precaution. If he, Hunter, carried out the task allotted him, then Yantze and Levin would remain in the background. Shadows within shadows. A menace lurking but unseen.

But how, from that covert surveillance, could they possibly know what he was up to?

Again Hunter grinned, but this time, as he nudged the bay with his heels and once more set off down the trail towards the Skillern tract, it was with elation not sadness. The War Between the States had been over for almost a year. For most of that time he had been drifting, in mind if not in body. Unable to settle. Unable to discard the Confederate army jacket that in a perverse way was a constant reminder of happier times. So was this business with Jarrow, and Yantze and Levin, the missing something he had been craving? Had it been the prospect of action that had driven him to make the insane decision to rob a bank, with the desire to help his mother rise from the depths of poverty just a convenient excuse? And was he now reluctant to put spurs to the big bay, and many miles between him and the town of

Nacogdoches, because the kick of a pistol butt against his palm and the reek of gunsmoke and blood inside a small town bank had set his senses singing and made him feel alive and of some use for the first time in many, many months?

Very likely, Hunter admitted. And even as the thought crossed his mind he saw ahead of him, above the trees and etched against the darkening eastern skies, the skeletal shape of Lyne Taliaferro Barret's oil derrick.

The cocking of the shotgun was a sharp, oily click in the evening stillness. For a moment the stillness held, became the breathless hush before the breaking of a storm. Then a man stepped out of the deep shadows at the side of the rough cabin. The cocked shotgun was held cradled in the crook of his right arm. Both his thumbs were hooked in the suspenders of his badly soiled bib overalls. His blue eyes were as clear and bright as summer skies. The look on his face was one of curiosity as he gazed at Hunter on the big bay.

'Heard about that ruckus in town. Rumour is a killer gunned down McCrae in the bank then stepped into his boots while they were still warm. Marshal Zac Hunter.' He shook his head in disbelief. 'Wondered when you'd get out here, what you'd look like.'

'And now you know,' Hunter said.

'But I don't know what you want, Hunter, and I don't much care. Why don't you just turn around and get the hell out of here? That badge is tarnished, those boots you stepped into are the wrong fit and you're not fit to lick them.'

'Are you Lyne Barret?'

'Yes, I'm Barret, and I want you off my land.'

'Pity. I had you down for a man of intelligence.'

'What the hell's that mean?'

'I've not met an intelligent man yet who'd put his faith in rumours that reach him third or fifth hand.'

'First hand. Ben Hollingsworth was in town very early today.'

'One of your partners.' Hunter nodded his understanding. 'In town, but not in the bank. That's how much of the truth he knows.'

'He's got eyes and ears. He heard the shooting, saw Jarrow run across the square with Quint. Word around town is you walked into the bank when your partners got into difficulties, and you killed McCrae.'

'If it's a rumour, treat it with contempt,' Hunter said. 'If the word was spread by Morgan Jarrow, the same applies: he's lying.'

The timbers of the derrick loomed like a large scaffold against the sky behind Hunter. He had ridden in from the trail, taken a look at the long, low building that would have been a bunkhouse on a different property and from whose lighted windows he could hear muffled talk and laughter. Then he had turned his attention instead to the cabin that was some distance away and set back against the woods. A lighted window. No sound. No sign of life.

Assuming there was one building for the workers, another for Barret and his co-directors, he had made that smaller cabin his goal. He'd walked the bay across the much-trampled clearing littered with tools and steel piping and off-cuts of timber, ridden past the tall structure, glanced fleetingly inside the derrick's framework and seen the glitter of a steel shaft, the black pulley belts connected to a steam engine. Pistons and connecting rods were standing still and silent, but he had smelt oil and lingering steam and, even from a several yards away, his face had been touched by the heat coming in waves from the surface of the copper boiler.

Suddenly, having carefully weighed his statement, Lyne Barret was nodding.

'Those very same thoughts did trouble me some. Alongside it came the thought that if Jarrow lied to the people of Nacogdoches about what went on in the bank, he's probably lied to you. That makes me curious about your intentions here; about what exactly Jarrow wants you to say to me.'

'Coffee,' Hunter said, 'would lubricate the vocal cords.'

Barret's gaze was shrewd.

'You realize if you came from Jarrow you probably had company on your ride?'

'All the more reason for us to talk inside.'

Without a word Barret turned on his heel and headed for the cabin. Hunter swung down from the bay and left it ground-hitched in the gathering gloom. Light from several oil lamps spilled over the step as he followed Barret and found himself inside a large, square room.

The first thing that struck him was the rack of gleaming Winchesters and shotguns against the back wall. He watched Barret walk over, ease the cock on the shotgun he was carrying and stand it in its allotted place, then turned his attention to a room that was, he realized, mostly office. Several dilapidated stuffed chairs were placed randomly, but desks littered with blueprints and thick manila folders, pens, ink wells and a whiskey bottle and several glasses, formed a U-shape dominating the centre of the room. There were three swivel chairs in the enclosure, two of them unoccupied. In the other a man was sitting. He had turned and sat up straight as Barret walked in. Now he was studying Hunter as he closed the cabin door.

'This is John Flint, another of my colleagues,' Barret said, by way of introduction. 'If you've noticed the badge, John, you'll know who this is.'

The chair creaked as the big man with a stubborn jaw and belligerent gaze sat back and stretched his legs.

'What's he want here?'

'Marshal Hunter's got a message for us from Morgan Jarrow,' Barret said. He hitched himself up onto one of the desks and sat with his hands clamped on the edge, legs dangling. 'Ain't that right, Marshal?'

'Not directly. It came from Tyne Coburn.'

'Ah.' Barret's sniff made his feelings evident. 'That makes it a legal matter.'

'Yes. According to Coburn, you're drilling for oil on sacred Indian land.'

Barret grinned in amazement. 'That's bullshit.'

The chair creaked again as John Flint hoisted his bulk erect. He reached across for the whiskey bottle, used three fingers to drag glasses towards him and poured three stiff drinks. He handed one to Barret, picked up the second and slid the third towards Hunter.

'The Indians have used this land for centuries,' he said. 'That's what brought us here. The oil's so close to the surface those fellows used to skim the black stuff off pools and water holes and use it as salve. I'll betcha they also used it when they braided their hair, used it to grease weapons.' He shrugged. 'As for religion, sacred ground – forget it.'

'I'm inclined to agree,' Hunter said equably.

Flint frowned. 'Yet you still went along with Jarrow's wishes and delivered the message.'

'It's complicated. Let's say that man's interpretation of events in the bank, and his none too subtle threats, left me with little choice.'

'Threats based on those lies we were talking about?' Flint smiled bleakly. 'If that's what you mean, then surely that little choice comes down to putting a lot of miles between you and Nacogdoches. Why not just keep on riding?'

'Because now I'm intrigued. The unpalatable truth is I rode into Nacogdoches, alone, to rob a bank. Why I had that intention is for me to worry about, though my admission does mean there's a grain of truth in those rumours. But what I walked into changed everything. A badge was pinned on my chest by a man who wants to be rich. I met a deputy who's not what he seems. A lawyer I know to be a deserter from the Army of the Confederacy sends me out into the night with a cock and bull story—'

The door banged open. A big man charged in. His

fists were clenched, his face suffused with anger.

'I spotted a rider out there on the edge of the woods,' he said. 'Can't be sure, but I reckon it was that man Yantze. I swear he saw me watching him, yet he hung around bold as brass, as if daring me to walk out there, challenge him—'

He broke off, suddenly noticing Hunter.

'Who the hell's this?'

'Zac Hunter, Nacogdoches' new marshal,' Barret said easily. 'Don't worry about that rider out there. John spotted him earlier. He's probably shadowing our friend here.'

'Friend?' the newcomer said incredulously. 'Jarrow pinned that badge on Hunter after he'd gunned down McCrae. The pair of them are in cahoots.'

'No, you're wrong on both counts,' Hunter said, 'but that's by the by. What interests me is why Jarrow's name keeps popping out whenever anyone in this room opens their mouth. Has he got a history that everyone knows about but me?'

The newcomer directed his gaze at Barret.

'Talk to him, Lyne, and you're talking to the enemy. Get him out of here, now.'

Barret shook his head. 'Hunter, this is Ben Hollingsworth. He tends to get a mite hot under the collar more often than's good for him, understandably perhaps, because he's put a lot of cash into this venture.'

'I hear there's two more partners,' Hunter said. 'Where are they?'

'Charlie Hamilton and Johnny Earle are in New York.'

'After more cash,' Hollingsworth growled, letting the

62

door bang shut behind him as he strode across to the desk and splashed whiskey into a glass.

'We've all ploughed our life savings into this venture,' Barret said. 'Our families back home are united behind us, their strength drives us on, but they're going through difficult times. We know there's oil down there, but drilling for it is expensive beyond belief, getting a successful well up and running when we make the strike will cost the earth and the moon.' He smiled absently. 'Charlie and Johnny are out there hoping to raise funds by offering shares in what so far is an unattractive and financially strapped enterprise. If they don't succeed—'

'Even if they do it'll be a waste of time if Jarrow gets his way,' Hollingsworth said.

'Then tell me about it,' Hunter said. 'Tell me what you mean by that, what you know about Jarrow. I'm outnumbered here. If, afterwards, you decide you've said too much, well, that rack tells me I'm also out-gunned and there's plenty of scrub around here where a body could go missing.'

'Now there's a thought,' Ben Hollingsworth said, and for the first time a smile flickered around his thin lips.

'You heard of Edwin Drake?'

Hunter shook his head.

'How about Seneca Oil?'

Hunter smiled, and again shook his head at Barret's question. 'I've heard of the Melrose Petroleum Oil Company. I also know that company was formed recently, but you began drilling way back in 1859 and got interrupted by the war.'

'Too damn right we did. In 1859 we leased nearly three hundred acres from Lucy W. Skillern in an area known as Oil Springs – that's right here. We set up the operation, pointed the drills at the earth and woke up to discover we were six years older.'

'Older or not, we're back and in business,' John Flint said.

Barret grimaced, then shook off his obvious bitterness and pressed on.

'The Pennsylvania Rock Oil Company was founded by George Bissel and Jonathan Eveleth in Titusville,' he said. 'A slick discovered on a pool worked well as lamp fuel, and those two fellers saw possibilities. There was a bit of a fracas between partners, the first company foundered and Seneca Oil rose from the ashes. Edwin Drake bought stock, then he was hired by Bissel and Eveleth on a salary of a thousand dollars. His job was to investigate the various oil seeps on land owned by Seneca.'

Hunter nodded slowly, sipping his whiskey.

'When was this?'

'Back in 1858,' Hollingsworth said. He was still prowling restlessly, glass in hand as he wandered between desks and window, alternately drinking and peering out into the dusk. 'Drake was living in the American Hotel with his wife Laura and two kids.'

'The date that should really interest you,' Barret went on, 'is 27 August the following year.'

'The year you began drilling,' Hunter acknowledged. 'If you're saying you were inspired by Drake, he must have succeeded.'

'Sure he did. He struck oil that day, a Saturday. His methods were different. He used what they call cable-tool or percussion drilling, we work with an auger clamped to jointed pipe and driven by that steam engine you passed on your way in.' He shrugged. 'But none of that matters unless you're actively involved in oil exploration. Call it background information. But when Drake was doing all that hard work back then before the war, the only fly in the ointment was a man called Morgan Jarrow.'

'Ah.' Hunter exhaled softly. 'What did Jarrow do, cause trouble?'

'I don't know the details. Word is he tried to buy Drake's shares with counterfeit money. There was talk of another man in the background, the real brains behind what was clearly an attempted takeover. Apparently Jarrow used a pistol to back his demands when the share offer was shown to be bogus.' Barret shrugged his shoulders. 'Whatever methods were used they didn't work, because Drake was still in control when war broke out.'

'Two oil companies,' Hunter said. 'Both operations halted by the war, and either side of that war this Morgan Jarrow turns up and tries to muscle in. Well, he told me he wanted to get rich. Seems clear he wants to do it the easy way.'

Again Barret shrugged his shoulders. 'Back in those days his planning was out, and the war would have stopped him in his tracks just as it did us, even if he'd been organized.' He looked contemplatively at Hunter.

'I guess the easy way you mentioned is to wait until I strike oil, then move in . . . with armed men? Is that what you see Jarrow doing?'

'Thanks for putting the question to me,' Hunter said. 'After the stories you've heard about me, I'm flattered. My answer is that, yes, that's one way Jarrow could work it, if he doesn't mind waiting. He's also trying this nonsense about sacred Indian land. I don't think he expects that to scare you off, though if it does he'd simply walk in and boss the operation. Wouldn't be difficult. The workers have the necessary skills—'

'Yeah, but the boss is the one who has to fork out the cash,' Barret said. 'Has Jarrow got finance?'

'Probably not. I'm sure he was behind that failed bank robbery in Nacogdoches. He was banking on that raid succeeding and bringing him a heap of cash in a hurry.'

'OK, so the only way he can work this is to let Melrose Petroleum Oil find the oil for him, then take over. With the oil flowing he'll have speculators rushing to invest, banks falling over themselves to lend him cash.'

'And this time,' John Flint said, 'he will be organized.'

'What the hell's that mean?' said Hollingsworth.

'If he could send two armed men into a bank, he can do the same here, with a bigger force.'

'And as the six men working for us on this site have refused point blank to get involved in armed conflict,' Barret said for Hunter's benefit, 'that leaves the four directors – useless with guns, and two of those will be away a while longer unless they can raise the cash we need. Unless we get some help, there's just three of us willing to fight for what we've got. Frankly, I don't rate our chances.'

His words hung in the air as the silence lengthened. To Hunter, Barret's meaning was crystal clear. It was with a quickening of the pulse that he met Barret's level gaze, and nodded slowly.

NINE

It was with mixed feelings that Zac Hunter rode past the tall derrick that was now but a vague shape against the night skies, the still, silent steam engine with the dull gleam of copper and brass fittings, and pointed the big blood bay towards Nacogdoches. There was elation there, more than a little confusion, and some amazement at the speed that events were unfolding. He had ridden out of town following orders given to him by, in Hunter's opinion, a crooked lawyer acting for a power-hungry predator. He was riding back with a commitment to help in any way he could a group of men desperate to strike oil and be at the forefront of an industry that in the very near future was sure to change the United States, and the world.

Easing the tension on the reins as the big horse sure-footedly picked its way over the clearing's rough ground and found the trail, Hunter wondered what that made him? He had heard of undercover agents during the war, men who worked their way into the Confederacy while remaining loyal to the Union cause. Those courageous men had relayed information back to the generals that probably helped win battles. Here in Nacogdoches there was no war, but on a smaller scale the men prepared to use force to wrest the rights to the black oil from the rightful owners were no less dangerous than those opposing armies.

A pale moon had emerged from behind thin cloud. The trail was bathed in an eerie half light, but visibility was down to less than fifty yards because of the wooded nature of the terrain. Unconcerned by Hollingsworth's sighting of the gunslinger Yantze – Hunter had, as far as Yantze would be able to tell, followed orders to the letter – he pushed on through the balmy, scented air with a strange feeling of contentment.

Yes, there was still concern for his mother, but there was also the strong sense of being involved in something useful, even of great importance, for the first time since the war. Part of that contentment came from the knowledge that he was now involved with hard-working men of honour. Barret and his colleagues had knowledge of Jarrow's villainy stretching back more than eight years. The man's move into Nacogdoches in May had been the start of a campaign aimed at undoing all their hard work. If Hunter could help prevent that . . . well, the satisfaction would be immense, and the rewards being offered by Lyne Barret for his assistance would enable Hunter's mother to live the rest of her life in comfort.

He'd set out to rob a bank, Hunter reflected, but in just in a few short hours his life had been turned around in a way he couldn't have imagined. And he was still basking in the glow of his unexpected good fortune when there was a dazzling flash in the woods to his right. It was followed by the crack of a rifle. As he ducked instinctively, a bullet hummed uncomfortably close to his ear.

The bay reacted like lightning. It slid to a halt on stiff legs, then spun as if to bolt back down the trail. Hunter held it with his fist twisted in tight reins, used his knees to hold it steady as he went for his six-gun. A second shot cracked. That bullet went wide. The element of surprise had gone. The bushwhacker's first killing shot had failed, the second was snatched too hurriedly. There was a hiatus, then he tried again. The third shot was much closer. Like a thorn snagging the material, it plucked at Hunter's shirt.

But the flashes had revealed the gunman's position. Jaw tight, Hunter put spurs to the reluctant bay and drove it straight at the trees. He charged into shadows cast by the sliver of moon, fired blind into the pitch darkness. The two shots were snapped rapidly with the sole aim of drilling uncertainty and terror into the mind of the bushwhacker. Hunter heard the bullets snick through the branches. He pulled back the bay fearful of injuring himself and the horse. Pistol tilted high, he listened with disbelief as a man breathed hoarsely, close by.

Then, as the big bay fought against Hunter's hold and surged forward, the rifle cracked again. A tremendous blow struck Hunter on the forehead. He felt himself falling, floating and, as he toppled from his horse, the last thing Hunter remembered was the sound of crashing in the undergrowth as the bushwhacker made his escape.

TEN

That's the stink of hides, of fresh animal skins Hunter thought, rolling his head, trying not to breathe. *And what the hell's that weird gurgling? Goddammit, I've been taken by Indians.*

The heat was oppressive. The stench was making him feel sick.

Cautiously, he opened his eyelids to thin slits. Through the blurred vision they offered he saw that he was in a rough cabin, looking up at the straw and cobwebs dangling from a sod roof. The skins he could smell were stretched on the raw timber walls, fixed with nails. He moved his head again, wincing as this time pain knifed through his skull, closed his eyes for a moment then opened them to take in details of the small, square room.

An oil lamp, the smoke of which was adding to the stench, showed him a clutter of tables and chairs, tin-types and calendars turning brown with age tacked to the walls between the rough hides. An iron stove that was the source of the heat stood glowing against a side wall. On its top there was a smoke-blackened coffee pot which explained the gurgling. An old Henry rifle stood against one of the tables on which lay, carelessly placed, a well-worn buffalo gun, a Colt Paterson belt pistol and several dirty tin plates. Against the back wall Hunter could see a crude cot. On it there was a tumble of faded Indian blankets.

He closed his eyes, and swallowed.

When he opened them again, a big man was standing looking down at him. A white man. Broad of shoulder, he was wearing a buckskin jacket, a broad leather belt with a big Bowie knife thrust into it, rough serge trousers tucked into boots as soft as moccasins. His long grey hair was tied back with a rawhide thong. His blue eyes were speculative.

Look at him, put two and two together, Hunter thought. Skins on the walls and the clothes he wore identified this man as a trapper. Preferable to Indians, but what did the speculative look mean? Was he wondering if he should finish the job? Wondering if Hunter's skin would fetch a good price.

Despite the pain, Hunter grinned.

'You see something funny?'

'I think I've made your day,' Hunter said, his voice coming thickly. 'From the look of those skins the most you can hope for in these parts is squirrels and rabbits, maybe a bob cat or a coyote. Today you got the king of the beasts.'

'Son, the last shot you heard before you blacked out was mine for sure, but it wasn't aimed your way. I saw what was going on. That coward who bushwhacked you

73

didn't much like the feel of a Sharps .50-.90 slug whistling close to his ear.'

'If that last shot was aimed some place else,' Hunter said, 'what knocked me out of the saddle?'

'Your horse moved, son. You remember that? He went too fast under a stout bough that was way too low. You didn't make it. The fresh lump on the side of your head goes well with the bruised jaw.'

This time Hunter laughed out loud, and managed a disbelieving shake of his head.

'Then I'm indebted to you twice over. You saved my bacon by scaring off that gunman, then brought me here to recover.' He hesitated, frowning. 'Here being where, exactly?'

'The foothills on the western edge of the Skillern tract.'

'How did we get here? How did I get here?'

'Belly down,' the big man said. 'Your horse is out back, fed and watered.'

Hunter nodded his thanks. 'Is this place close to Barret's drillings?'

'I get a clear view in daylight. That would have put me close enough to hear the shooting and get to you before it was too late. As it happens, I didn't need to do that.'

'Whatever *was* required of you, you did it and thank God for that,' Hunter said fervently. He struggled to a sitting position. He had been lying on a second crude cot tight up against a side wall. With a grunt of effort he swung his feet to the dirt floor and extended his hand. 'My name's Zac Hunter. I heartily thank you for what you've done.'

'I know who you are, son, even without the badge,' the big trapper said. He took Hunter's hand, squeezed it with a grip of iron and for the first time the beginnings of a smile creased his weather-beaten face. 'My names Gregor McCrae. If that rings a bell, it's because I'm big Danny McCrae's kid-brother.'

'If I believed it was you killed Danny,' McCrae said affably, 'you wouldn't have experienced the pleasure of shaking my hand because you'd be lying out there in the scrub with my .50-.90 slug buried deep in your brain.'

Hunter was puzzled.

'Most people in Nacogdoches are listening to rumours that brand me a killer. You live out here in the woods, hunt for your food. I'd expect you to know nothing of recent events, yet you know your brother's been shot dead, and you don't believe I'm responsible. How can that be? Either the truth travels fast and in mysterious ways, or there's something I'm not understanding.'

'I was in town most of the day. If you think back you'll recall seeing me outside the barber shop when you rode in. I was intrigued by your manner. That made me put off my monthly shave until later. I followed you to the square, lazed in the sun for a while ruminating on this and that, then caught up with you again later when I was clean shaven and you were leaving the jail office. You could say I know more about what's been going on than you do.'

Hunter took a sip of the hot coffee, looked at McCrae over the tin cup's rim. 'Then you being there, close enough to rescue me, wasn't a stroke of luck?'

McCrae shrugged. 'Sharp ears, sharp eyes, an inquisitive mind – and I had work to do.'

'And your brother's dead,' Hunter said quietly.

'We weren't close, but still it hurts like hell. I admired Danny; he didn't approve of the way I live my life, but we had come to terms with the differences and were comfortable with each other. And, yes, my being in the right place when you were attacked really was happenstance. I said I had work to do. I was checking a string of traps, and that happened to put me close by and watching when you came to the end of your ride. No barber's shop this time, and you didn't see me. But I was there, in thick timber on the other side of the drillings. I saw you go in with Barret, saw Hollingsworth spot that rider who'd been shadowing you and charge into the cabin like a bull.'

'D'you get close?'

McCrae shook his head. 'Not close enough to hear. Walls are thick.' He smiled. 'Like I said, your demeanour in town intrigued me. Watching people is a kind of hobby. I suppose that comes from watching the way animals behave the better to understand them.' He savoured that idea for a moment, then said, 'I know you went into Barret's cabin in one frame of mind, came out feeling entirely different. You're about to tell me why.'

Hunter put his empty cup on the table close to the blued barrel of the big Sharps buffalo gun that had saved his life. He lifted his arms, stretched, touched the swelling above his right ear, waggled his jaw, tongued the tooth broken by Morgan Jarrow. Then he strolled across to the window and stood looking out across the moonlit clearing and the grass sloping down to the trees.

'It's complicated,' he said, 'but this is the way I see it. Nacogdoches is a small town, small population, nobody with grand ambitions. That made it easy for Morgan Jarrow to seize power back in May. Since then he's hired himself two gunslingers, and he's been surrounding himself with men who will do his bidding, without question. Your brother wouldn't play ball. Jarrow arranged a bank robbery with the twin aims of raising cash and getting rid of Marshal Dan McCrae. Your brother was gunned down, but then I appeared out of nowhere and the bank robbery was doomed. Now, because there were no witnesses to what happened in the bank, Jarrow believes he has some kind of a hold on me.'

'Seems straightforward enough to me,' McCrae said.

Hunter turned back to the room. McCrae was sitting by the table, idly polishing the barrel of the Sharps with a cloth.

'Go on.'

'Not much to say: you've already worked out this is all about oil.'

Hunter nodded. 'Jarrow went after another oil company several years ago, in Pennsylvania. Whatever he tried wasn't enough. This time he's planned well. The law's thin on the ground in these parts, and he sees himself with a pet lawyer, me in his pocket and townsfolk too complacent ever to be a threat. If there is a stirring of discontent, I'm sure his tame councillor, Strachan, will make sure it's quashed.'

'Don't underestimate that man.'

'Strachan?' Hunter found it difficult not to laugh. 'He charged into the bank with Jarrow. A less imposing figure I have yet to meet.'

'Nevertheless,' McCrae said, 'a newspaper editor who prints the truth must be prepared to reason with irate citizens, face down those threatening him with violence – and Bart Strachan's been doing that, with dignity and strength, for many years.'

'I'm surprised,' Hunter admitted. 'However, the point I was about to make still stands: if there is discontent it will come to nothing. Morgan Jarrow can make a move on Barret at a time of his choosing, with the certainty of being unopposed.'

'Best time, easiest time,' McCrae said, 'would be when Barret hits the jackpot. Them and their drillers'd be flying high, over the moon with excitement. Jarrow's gunslingers could stroll in and shoot 'em down like ducks.'

'Sure, but no matter which way he plays it he's backed a winner. If Jarrow leaves Barret to manage the oil well, the town profits – and Jarrow already owns the town. But my hunch is Jarrow wanted to go in now, fast and hard. To do that he needed cash to pay the drillers.'

McCrae smiled. 'Happenstance again. You walked into the bank and ruined his plans. But what about Lyne Taliaferro Barret? I said you walked out of his cabin with a spring in your step, looking like the cat who'd found the cream. What the hell happened in there, son?'

'What I found was a cause,' Hunter said, with absolute conviction. 'Those five men running the Melrose Petroleum Oil Company are staking everything they've got on a venture that can change the world. If it fails they go bust, their families starve, and a man not fit to polish their boots is planning an illegal and violent takeover.'

'And Barret's asked for your help? You're the knight in shining armour who's going to ride to the rescue?'

'If by so doing I can bring down the man I'm certain is behind your brother's murder – is that a bad thing?'

McCrae grimaced. He'd finished polishing the Sharps. Now he screwed up the rag and tossed it onto the clutter of Indian blankets on his cot. He lifted the big buffalo gun to his shoulder, looked along the sights to the window and gently put pressure on the trigger.

'Pow,' he said softly – then looked at Hunter and shook his head.

'You said it was complicated. You'd better store that remark for future reference and keep your eyes wide open at all times. Morgan Jarrow may have more cunning than you give him credit for – if credit's the right word. On the surface this takeover of Barret's fledgling oil company – whatever form it takes – is straightforward, like I said. But supposing Jarrow's playing this like stud poker, with a powerful hole card in reserve?'

'If he is, that makes two of us. You know Quint?'

Suddenly distracted, McCrae frowned. Then he said, 'Sure. Ended up another of Jarrow's men. Rode into town and took the deputy's badge. My brother pinned it on him, but with some reluctance.'

'Quint,' Hunter said, 'is my hole card.'

McCrae's eyes widened. 'You're not serious. Would you mind explaining that?'

'Nope. If I did, he'd no longer be my ace in the hole. However, I am wondering where you got this idea that Jarrow's playing his cards close to his chest.'

'May be nothing,' McCrae said, and he leaned sideways and stood the Sharps in a crude wooden rack nailed to the wall. 'I'm a trapper, a woodsman. I cover a lot of ground, at all hours of the day and night. And I can tell you now that a couple of fellows with enough weaponry to start a war are living in a permanent camp on a creek a few miles west of here.' He winked at Hunter. 'They've been out there ever since Morgan Jarrow rode in and took over Nacogdoches.'

ELEVEN

It was almost midnight. Morgan Jarrow, sitting at a table in the Old Colonial with a glass of beer in front of him, flicked his eyes to the left as the door banged open and Yantze strode in. The tall, grey-haired gunman made straight for the bar, poured whiskey from a bottle pushed towards him by Cobb, the saloonist, then headed for Jarrow's table. He sat, tasted his drink, then put it down with the delicacy of a gent settling a china cup in its saucer. Only then did he look at Jarrow.

'Someone took a shot at our lawman.'

Jarrow frowned. 'Barret's doing? They drove him off?'

'No, Hunter was in the Melrose cabin so long him and Barret must have got right friendly. This happened when Hunter left and was heading this way. He was bushwhacked.'

'Someone took a shot at him, you said. That sounds like he got away.'

Ignoring what was obviously a question, Yantze tasted his drink again, then drained it and turned to waggle the empty glass at Cobb. The scar on his face seemed

81

emphasized by the low light, giving him a sinister appearance. He stroked his moustache, waited in silence. The fresh drink was brought to him by the aproned saloonist. Yantze drank half, taking his time, while Jarrow fumed with impatience.

'I was some ways off by then,' Yantze continued, eyes lowered as if talking to his glass. 'Hunter had left the drillings and I was done with being nursemaid. Then I heard shots, the crack of a rifle. A crashing in the undergrowth. An almighty bang that sounded like a cannon going off. Then silence.'

'And? You mean there's no more, that's it?'

'Not quite. I worked my way closer, keeping to the shadows. That big bay of Hunter's was out in the open, quivering in the moonlight. No sign of Hunter. Then a man tall as a tree, wide as a door, came crashing backwards out of the timber, dragging our friend. With some effort he heaved him up so he was belly down across the saddle.'

He was watching Jarrow now, watching the ever-changing emotions flickering across his tense face, deliberately inserting pauses to drag out his tale.

'For Christ's sake,' Jarrow hissed.

Yantze smiled, crinkling the scar.

'This fellow led the bay, Hunter flopping loose across the saddle, back through the woods. Must have been to where his own horse was tethered. A short while later I heard two horses being ridden away from there.'

Jarrow sat back. He was frowning, trying to make sense of what Yantze had told him. He shook his head.

'How do you read it? Was the man who took Hunter

82

the bushwhacker?'

Yantze shrugged his shoulders.

'If that man was the bushwhacker,' Jarrow went on, 'who the hell is he, and what's he up to?'

'And if he wasn't,' Yantze said, 'then same question has to be asked – only twice over. I heard two different weapons: a rifle, then a gun powerful enough to drop a buffalo in its tracks. Two weapons that different, with shots coming that close together, has to mean two men. So who are they?'

'*Where* are they?' Jarrow said. 'And where is Hunter?'

Yantze was nodding slowly, his eyes hooded.

'That's something you'd better find out, and fast,' he said. 'From where I'm sitting, it looks like putting your trust in Zac Hunter is one of those decisions you'll spend the rest of your life regretting.' He grinned. 'Always supposing you live long enough to have regrets.'

Fifteen minutes later, midnight come and gone. Yantze had left soon after his chilling parting shot. Morgan Jarrow had spent those fifteen minutes brooding into his empty glass. He was cogitating on the planning he had done, the steps he had taken, and wondering if Yantze was right; if taking on Zac Hunter had been a bad move and, if so, how many more decisions he would live to regret.

The Old Colonial was almost empty. Jarrow stood up and scuffed his boots through thin sawdust on his way to the bar. Cobb was behind the bar, tidying up. Dark eyes under heavy black brows looked at Jarrow. The saloonist wiped his hands on the grubby apron tied around his massive paunch, then walked closer to Jarrow and leaned stiff-armed on the timber bar.

'Strachan was in the back room earlier today.'

'Am I supposed to be impressed?'

'He was in there a couple of hours, talking to three cronies.'

Suddenly Jarrow was listening intently.

'Go on.'

Cobb grinned. 'Don't need to, do I? Jake Rogers, Frank Leland, Sol Cotter. Those names set bells ringing?'

Jarrow's face was bleak. 'I dismissed all three from the council.'

'But not Strachan.' Cobb straightened up, spread his hands, his dark eyes unreadable. 'Three ex-members of Nacogdoches' town council meet with the editor of the town newspaper and ask for privacy, no intruders,' he said. 'But so what? They're entitled. Peace and quiet. A bottle, four glasses. Why should something so goddamn ordinary be a cause for concern?'

'Nobody said that it was,' Jarrow said through his teeth. He thought for a moment, then said, 'Who booked the room, which one of them insisted on privacy?'

'Insisted,' Cobb shook his head. 'Can't remember any insistence; can't remember anything much other than what I've told you.'

'For Christ's sake,' Jarrow said fiercely, 'has the sun fried your brains—?'

'I said I can't remember,' Cobb said bluntly, as he walked away, 'and I'd be grateful if you'd shut the door on your way out.'

*

The light was still burning in Tyne Coburn's office when Jarrow swung down from his horse, hitched it to the rail and banged on the door. Impatiently he waited, listening to muted clattering, the scrape of a chair. The door was flung open, revealing the lawyer. Coburn's string tie was hanging loose. His black jacket was unbuttoned, and wrinkled. He was rocking on heels and toes. A cigar was smouldering in his fist as he glared out at Jarrow. Over the lawyer's shoulder Jarrow could see light from the oil lamp on the desk flooding over a smeared glass and almost empty whiskey bottle.

'We've got trouble,' Jarrow said and, without waiting for a reply, he shouldered past Coburn and strode into the room. He waited there, his body moving restlessly, shifting his feet. The door slammed. Coburn walked around him, around the desk, and slumped into his swivel chair.

'We've been through this once,' he said, his voice hoarse from too much smoke and strong drink. 'You get involved with a man you know nothing about, a violent, dangerous man—'

'Not Hunter,' Jarrow said impatiently. 'Strachan and the council members I kicked out got together in Cobb's back room. Asked for privacy, didn't want to be disturbed. According to Cobb they were in there a couple of hours. They've all got businesses to run, yet they took time out – a lot of time.'

Coburn's pockmarked face held a sheen of sweat. He flicked ash into a hollowed buffalo hoof, looked at the whiskey and ran his tongue over his plump lips.

'Why is that trouble? Those fellows know what happened today, they know McCrae was gunned down and a man of your choosing appointed marshal; a man who downed two bank robbers as easy as swatting flies. If they had notions of getting rid of you, of getting their old jobs back, those hopes have been dashed. Today you strengthened your hold on Nacogdoches, Jarrow. All they were doing was drowning their sorrows.'

'No.' Jarrow shook his head, found another glass on the desk and splashed into it a large measure of the strong spirits. 'Five months ago, I hit three of them hard. *That's* when they drowned their sorrows. But time heals wounds. Simmering discontent can too easily turn to anger. After five months, what happened to them is a bad dream. Now they want action.'

'Who does?' Coburn said. 'All four I suppose, if you're right – but who's the ringleader? Not Strachan; you kept Strachan on the council because he runs the newspaper and could be dangerous, but you were thinking of the printed word and I can't see him going against you in any physical sense. Nor can I see him leading a coup. So think hard, name your man, then go after him and you nip this in the bud.'

Jarrow was frowning, pacing like an animal caged. Whiskey spilled from the forgotten glass. Irritably he shifted it to his other hand and with a grimace licked his wet palm. He stopped, swung to face Coburn.

'Sol Cotter's too old.'

Coburn shook his head. 'Cotter's fought in two wars that I know of. He's a cantankerous old coot and he's got nothing to lose. Cotter's a possibility.'

'What about Jake Rogers?'

'A shifty character. Oily. If he's doing the organizing, I wouldn't work under him. If I was head man, I wouldn't want him on the team.'

Jarrow narrowed his eyes, pursed his lips thoughtfully as he sank down into one of the easy chairs.

'If it's a choice between Cotter and Frank Leland,' he said softly, 'then in my opinion it's no contest.'

'You saying Leland's behind this?'

Smoke from Coburn's cigar curled around the hot lamp glass and was carried towards the ceiling. Jarrow leaned back, watching it. The glass tilted slackly in his hand. His eyes were hooded.

'Leland,' he said – and he nodded. 'Yes, it's Leland.'

'Get rid of him,' Coburn said. 'Tonight.'

TWELVE

Frank Leland took most of his meals in the town's café, and lived alone above his gunsmith's shop on Main Street. Since the death of his wife he rarely went to bed early, and after a day that had seen Nacogdoches torn by the bloody battle in the bank that ended in the death of a respected marshal, his mind refused to give up its relentless churning – churning, moreover, that he knew was getting him nowhere.

So he remained in his comfortable living room, stripped to his pants and undershirt, looking down over Nacogdoches as the hustle and bustle of a busy small town died away and everywhere the oil lamps were lowered or extinguished.

Except, that was, for those in Cobb's saloon.

It was with considerable interest that Leland noticed the lamps still glowing, for they had been drawn to his attention when the man called Yantze rode into town, tied his lathered horse at the rail and pushed his way into the saloon. One horse was already hitched there, a roan whose vaguely familiar image kept poking at Leland's memory without much effect.

Yantze remained inside for some time. Leland kept a careful watch, darting frequently to the window while brewing coffee, standing in the cover of the faded curtains as he drank the hot black java.

Eventually, after half an hour or so, he had watched Yantze emerge, haloed by the lamplight flooding the street, and ride across to the livery barn to stable his horse. From there he'd walked to the rooming-house where he spent his nights.

Kept at his post by a nagging suspicion that there was more to come, Leland narrowed his eyes in thought when a short while later Morgan Jarrow stormed out of the saloon. The leader of the town council untied his horse, flung himself into the saddle and rode off down the street in a cloud of dust.

All right, Leland thought, so that's why I recognized the roan. But what the hell were those two talking about? Yantze rode into town, his horse looking the worse for wear. Jarrow was already in Cobb's place. So, they met, shared a drink, chewed the fat – nothing unusual in that, no cause for alarm.

But these were no ordinary men, Leland mused. Yantze was a hired gunman. Jarrow was the man paying his wages. Yet even those two facts did not lend a sinister import to their late-night drink in Cobb's saloon were it not for a third fact that Leland knew he could not ignore.

On his way to the meeting in Cobb's back room, Leland had seen Yantze riding out of town in an easterly direction. And as he crossed the street to the saloon,

Leland had watched with interest as Marshal Zac Hunter
cantered up the street before the dust of the gunman's
passing had settled.

Yantze was back in town. Hunter – as far as Leland
knew – was not.

It was with a worried frown creasing his brow that the
gunsmith at last left his post at the window, blew out the
lamp and climbed into bed.

The moon had slipped behind heavy black clouds. It was
that miserable time between midnight and dawn when,
even in early autumn, cold gnaws through to chill the
bones and the spirits sink to their lowest ebb. It was a
time carefully chosen by the tall figure who slipped
through the shadows at the inner edge of the plank walk
and with a gloved hand tried the handle of Frank
Leland's shop door.

The door was locked.

Slow, patient movement. A knife blade glittered in the
gloom. There was the barely audible crunch of wood
splintering, a click that brought the intruder's head
jerking around in alarm.

Nothing stirred. Somewhere out in the woods a big cat
howled. Down the street, in the livery barn, a horse softly
whickered.

Leland's front door swung open. The tall man slipped
inside. He crept across the shop floor to the counter, the
smell of gun oil in his nostrils, slipped silently past the
counter to the door leading to the back room and from
there to the stairs leading to Leland's living-quarters.

On his way up, a stair creaked. The man's intake of

breath was sharp in the deathly silence. He waited, listening, then climbed the rest of the way to the narrow landing illuminated by faint light entering through a small window. Again he paused to listen.

Then he smiled.

Behind one of the doors on the landing, a man was snoring.

This door was not locked.

Confident now, the tall man let himself into the bedroom and for a moment stood there inhaling the masculine scents while his eyes adjusted to the deeper gloom. In time he could make out the narrow cot, the shape of the man who was lying there snoring. On his back. Arms out-flung. Mouth agape.

In one swift movement the intruder stepped forward, lifted the knife that had been in his hand ever since he had broken into the shop, and brought it down hard and fast to plunge with a sickening sound into the breast of the sleeping man.

PART TWO

THIRTEEN

11 September, 1866

Hunter's ride back into Nacogdoches from Gregor
McCrae's cabin took him past the Melrose Petroleum Oil
Company's Skillern tract site. It was a warm, wet
September morning, heavy rain falling steadily from
sullen grey skies. As Hunter rode by the drillings, his
horse splashing through standing pools, he could hear
the clatter and hiss of the steam engine, the thump and
grind of the drill, and in his imagination felt the ground
trembling beneath the big blood bay's hoofs. Workmen
in muddy boots and oilskin capes slick with rain watched
him without pausing in their tasks. He saw a big
workman with an air of authority who was barking orders
even as he fixed Hunter with a baleful glare; another
man he thought could be Barret and towards whom he
directed a friendly wave before continuing on his way.

For a while the big workman lingered in Hunter's

memory, the fierce look on the man's face vaguely menacing, certainly unexpected, unexplained and, Hunter thought, uncalled for. Then he shook his head, irritated by what seemed already to be an irrational obsession with trivia.

On either side of the trail the woods were thick, banking up in dark masses towards higher ground where the tops of the trees were lost in the trailing skirts of low cloud. Hunter pushed the bay to a fast canter, hunched in the saddle, his face wet under his pulled-down hat and his eyes constantly darting in all directions. He had been shot at out of darkness, his life saved only by a freak accident and the powerful roar of a trapper's heavy Sharps buffalo gun. The man who had wanted him dead could easily have followed McCrae and the unconscious Hunter to the cabin, spent a wet, uncomfortable night in the woods then picked up the trail again as Hunter rode out not long after dawn.

So Hunter proceeded towards town with his senses attuned to possible dangers tracking him across the murky, wooded terrain, at every moment expecting the crack of a rifle, the hum of a bullet; aware, with a sense of resignation, that if that bullet did howl through the moist air in his direction he would almost certainly hear nothing, feel nothing. In daylight, the gunman would carefully plant his first slug in the centre of Hunter's back.

But not that day. In an hour, ten miles passed beneath the big bay's hoofs without incident. The rain had eased by the time Hunter entered Nacogdoches' Main Street and made for the square, but his clothes were damp and he felt thoroughly miserable. His mood was not brightened when he caught sight of the buckboard standing outside the gunsmith's. Two men were struggling to carry a limp body out of the shop's narrow doorway and across the plank walk. Uncaring, they stood on the edge, took a couple of swings and flung the dead man into the wet buckboard. Hunter winced as the body thumped hard onto the boards, head flopping. The wagon rocked. The horse tossed its head in the traces and snorted.

Another killing, and this time I know the man, Hunter thought. *That's four men dead, and I've been here twenty-four hours.*

With a frown creasing his brow, his bruised head aching abominably, he rode across the square and dismounted outside the jail office. He was aware of people watching him from the bank as he tied the bay. Then he stamped into the office where Quint was sitting in front of the desk smoking and drinking coffee.

The deputy turned and looked up at Hunter, watched him as he strode across the room and stood spread-legged with his back to the hot stove, his hands behind his back.

'You're looking pale. You hit trouble out there?'

'Trouble hit me,' Hunter said, flexing his stiff fingers in the waves of heat. 'Looking after the office was the plum job, next time we'll draw straws.'

Quint's grin didn't reach his eyes. He didn't press Hunter for details of the trouble that had left the new marshal looking the worse for wear, and that, Hunter thought, was odd.

'You hear about Frank Leland?'

Hunter shook his head. 'I saw a body being carried out of the gunsmith's shop, if that's what you mean.'

'That was Leland. Someone broke into the place and slipped a knife between his ribs.'

'You're deputy town marshal. Why aren't you down there?'

'Sol Cotter trotted in here to report the killing. I went with Sol to Leland's place. The man was in his bed, cold and stiff. I got Sam Allman over there with his buckboard. Nothing more I could do.'

Hunter grunted, shifted his weight.

'Any ideas?'

Quint shrugged. 'I asked a few questions. Seems Leland attended a meeting in Cobb's place.'

'Cobb?'

'Runs the saloon.'

'What was the meeting?'

'Either those I questioned don't know, or they're close-mouthed. I do know it was in a back room, with the door shut.'

'Who was there?'

'Well, Leland that I know of—'

He broke off as the street door creaked fully open and an old man wearing work overalls and a faded felt hat stepped over the threshold. His boots were wet and caked with mud and he carried with him the stink of horses. His grey eyes lighted on Hunter.

When he took another step into the room, Hunter saw that he was not alone. The second man was . . . Bart Strachan, yes, he of the timid looks who had been ordered by Jarrow to get the buckboard for the dead men in the bank. But who, according to Gregor McCrae, had for a long time been the fearless editor of Nacogdoches' weekly newspaper.

And this was a noticeably different Strachan, Hunter thought, taking stock of the man's demeanour as he closed the door carefully behind him and stepped around the old man. Small in stature still, but now with a commanding presence. What had brought about such a radical change?

Strachan was watching him, traces of an understanding smile lurking.

'You're wondering what's going on? Well, what you saw in me yesterday was the character I needed to present to Morgan Jarrow. You see, I had that man weighed up from the day he rode into town, and I've carried the weight of that necessary pose for five months. It became wearisome.'

'That's Bart Strachan talking, newspaper editor and town councillor,' Quint said quietly. 'The old-timer's Sol Cotter; I guess you don't need telling he runs the livery barn.'

Hunter, still drying his clothes, nodded thoughtfully at the two men.

'So why change the pose now, Strachan?'

'One reason was that it no longer served its purpose. After five months in this town, Jarrow had heard enough talk to realize that the man he kept on the council was not only a wolf in sheep's clothing, he was the man with the means to bring him down.'

'The newspaper. The power of the written word.'

Strachan nodded. 'Then there's the second reason. Yesterday a new man hit town. You, Hunter. You hit it hard, and you hit fast. Two bank robbers died – and good riddance to them. A good lawman also died, but he was a hesitant man. Hesitancy doesn't appear to be in your make-up. I knew at once that yesterday everything had changed, there'd been a shift in power—'

'Circumstances can force a man to act out of character,' Hunter said. 'I was caught in a desperate situation, fighting for my life. Also, there were no witnesses to the three killings in the bank. Morgan Jarrow saw possibilities, now I'm over a barrel. You could say even if I'm the man you've been waiting for, my hands are tied.'

He raised his eyebrows, waited. The old man had sunk into a chair close to Quint, and now he was shaking his head.

'Could've rode away, any man would've,' he said. 'The fact you didn't sets you apart.' His grin showed pink gums. 'Jarrow smacked you in the teeth with his scattergun. I think that was a big mistake.'

Hunter nodded. 'A certain gent making his living out in the woods has got me down as a knight in shining armour. You seem to be expressing the same opinion. It's becoming an embarrassment, so before I'm overcome with emotion, would you two fellows mind getting to the point?'

'Morgan Jarrow's taken over Nacogdoches,' Strachan said. 'He managed it because this is a lazy East Texas town. He caught us all off guard, there was no opposition. When the time's right, he'll take over Lyne

Barret's oil company. He'll do that easy, too: Yantze and Levin up against hard-working mining engineers and businessmen'll be a massacre.'

'Just the businessmen,' Hunter said. 'I got it from Barret that those drillers will stand well back.'

'That makes a gloomy picture look even worse, but if we do side with the town, or with Barret – which is maybe the same thing – then the odds shift,' Quint said. 'That's what Strachan's after. He's appealing to you, but I've been in office here for five months and McCrae rated me highly. With both of us in, Jarrow's in trouble.'

Hunter grimaced, left the warmth of the stove and sat down at the desk.

'So what's the plan, Strachan? I hear there was a meeting in Cobb's place. Leland was there, now he's dead. You walking in here suggests you were not only at the meeting, but figured prominently.'

'I called the meeting. Both of us were there. You know about Leland. The fourth man there was the town's barber, Jake Rogers.'

'I'd like to know what was discussed, what decisions were made.'

'Just this,' Sol Cotter said. 'Talk to Zac Hunter. Sound him out. See if he's with us or agin us.'

'Some plan,' Hunter said scathingly, 'if that's all you could come up with.'

'There's torn stitching on that jacket you're wearing,' Strachan said, with a nod towards Hunter. 'I'd say it once bore the insignia of a Confederate Army officer. It fits well, which suggests it's not stolen. If you're in with us, then that kind of background says you do the planning.'

'Tyne Coburn was also an officer in the Confederate Army,' Hunter pointed out. 'If he's working for Morgan Jarrow, doesn't that create some kind of an impasse? Brother officers with identical training, similar plans meet head on and cancel each other out.'

Sol Cotter turned his head bald head and spat drily but eloquently.

Hunter grinned.

'You seem to have him weighed up, old-timer. Well, I can tell you now that Coburn's a deserter from the Confederacy turned shyster lawyer,' he went on, 'but he's still on the opposing side. And dishonourable conduct doesn't rule out a fine brain.'

'Opposing side,' Strachan murmured, liking the sound. 'Does that mean you're throwing your hat in with us?'

Hunter glanced at the deputy. 'Quint's already stated his allegiance. What I've just said merely underlined that Coburn's on the side opposing you fellows. Unlike Quint, before I make any decision on *my* position I need to know more; being cracked with Jarrow's shotgun didn't make me an instant hero. So there's this: four men were at that meeting, one's dead, two are here talking to me. Why two, when there should be three?'

Strachan and Cotter exchanged glances. Strachan sighed.

'When the meeting closed, there was a show of hands to determine commitment and unity.' He shook his head. 'Only three hands went up.'

FOURTEEN

Jake Rogers was making his way towards the café for a late breakfast fry-up when he noticed Strachan and Cotter entering the jail office and closing the door. He stopped well back on the opposite plank walk and stared across the square, brow furrowed. Unnoticed by Rogers, who was stunned by what he had seen, wagons and riders were grinding and splashing through the mud. Vapour from the horses' heaving flanks and flared nostrils rose to add to the damp mist that had settled over the town. The females of the town – ladies and working girls – were squealing and holding their skirts as mud sprayed from wagon wheels and the flashing hoofs of the horses.

Rogers found himself presented with a serious dilemma. His stomach was rumbling, and it was clear that more pressing business must come between him and his breakfast. In his heart, he believed that what he was about to do would be good for the town. Yet taking that one enormous step that would isolate him forever from his old way of life, and from his many friends, was suddenly proving more difficult than he could ever have imagined during his long night-hours of soul-searching. More difficult, for sure, than the decision not to raise his hand in Cobb's back room and join forces with Cotter, Strachan and Leland.

And it was the cruel killing of Leland, Rogers thought bleakly and with a genuine sense of loss, that was threatening to jolt him from his chosen path.

Yet even as those thoughts raced through his mind – and across the square the door to the jail office remained firmly closed – his feet were taking him in the direction of Main Street, and the office of the lawyer, Tyne Coburn. Why Coburn? Because, Jake Rogers reasoned, while the lawyer was no less dangerous than Morgan Jarrow, his temper was always held on a much tighter rein.

For Rogers was convinced that when he received the bad news, Morgan Jarrow was likely to explode.

When Jake Rogers hammered boldly on the door and was invited into Coburn's smoke-filled office, he saw at once that the lawyer was not alone. In one of the worn easy chairs recently occupied by Yantze and Levin, Morgan Jarrow was looking his most threatening. Coburn was in his usual position in the leather chair behind his oak desk. His fleshy, pockmarked face was pale, and the fingers holding the inevitable cigar were trembling.

Been drinking long into the night, Rogers opined, and he swallowed uncomfortably when he realized that would make even this man more dangerous, the temper less easily controlled. It was with that troubling thought that he flicked a glance towards the always less predictable Morgan Jarrow. The man was smiling. Somehow, that made him more chilling, and Rogers struggled to suppress a small shiver of fear.

'Welcome, Jake Rogers,' Jarrow said. 'While you're here, why don't you make yourself useful by attending to our friend behind the desk. He is a little unsteady. Rather than risk cutting his own throat while shaving—'

'My case is back in the shop, I've got no gear with me,' Rogers blurted.

'No,' Jarrow said. He swept Rogers with his contemptuous gaze. The smile that had never reached his cold eyes was now wiped from his face. 'But you've heard about Frank Leland, haven't you? He died by the knife and, as you were also in that group in Cobb's back room, you've come to plead for your miserable life. Well, you can rest easy. Leland was removed because without a leader the others will sneak off into the shadows with their tails between their legs—'

'The wrong man was murdered.'

That shocked Jarrow.

'The hell you say. Are you saying Leland wasn't top dog, didn't call that meeting?'

'That was Strachan. Strachan's calling the shots. Frank was' – Rogers swallowed and shook his head – 'he was just a hard man with a knowledge of weapons. As well as being one of us, that made him useful.'

'So if you're not here begging for mercy – what *do* you want?'

'I saw Strachan and Cotter. They're over at the jail now, talking to Zac Hunter.'

The words came out in a rush. Rogers had anticipated a strong reaction, and it came, but the cause was unexpected.

Jarrow was up out the chair in a flash, his brows knitted.

'Hunter?' he said. 'You telling me he's back in town?'

'Didn't know he'd left. Yeah, he's in there – leastwise, that big horse of his is tied to the rail.'

'You haven't seen him? You don't know if he's fit and well, injured?'

Rogers, still standing by the door, was frowning, utterly confused.

'Leave it,' Tyne Coburn said bluntly to Jarrow. 'Think about what the man said: Strachan and Cotter are talking to Hunter. That spells trouble. Whatever it is went on in that back room's been taken a step further.'

'What did go on in there, Rogers?' Jarrow said through clenched teeth. 'Is there some kind of uprising being planned, a plot to bring me down—'

'Only thing we decided was to talk to Hunter,' Rogers cut in hurriedly. 'No, that's not right. It was them decided. There was a show of hands, and I kept well out of it.'

'Very sensible,' Coburn said, 'but how far are you prepared to go? You've distanced yourself from your remaining friends. Does that mean you're aligned with us? Will you go so far as to use a weapon against the opposition?'

Rogers' head was whirling.

'I . . . suppose so,' he said, a quiver in his voice. 'Yes – if that's what it comes to, then I will, because it'll be for the good of the town.'

He had closed his eyes as the words left his lips, and so he missed the swift exchange of glances between Jarrow and Coburn.

'Yantze and Levin, you and me, Tyne – and now Rogers.' Jarrow was speaking softly, almost to himself. 'That's four, for certain. We could do with more, but. . . .' His eyes cleared, and he looked directly at Coburn. 'Move now, or sit tight and wait?' He grinned wolfishly. 'Looks to me like it's decision time.'

Rogers had gone. Not exactly sneaking out like a whipped dog, Jarrow thought, but with the air of a defeated man looking without hope into a bleak future.

'I don't trust that man,' he said to Coburn.

'Forget him. If he changes horses again, he's no great loss and can do us no harm. Concentrate on Zac Hunter and the other two, Strachan and Sol Cotter. Particularly Strachan. You knew he was a danger. If he showed weakness in his dealings with you, it was a clever ploy. He was and is the enemy in the tent, Jarrow, and now Leland's death has alerted him to real danger he'll be on his guard.'

'Damn him,' Jarrow said fiercely. 'I kept that man on—'

'Because you thought he'd be useful and, deep down, you feared him,' Coburn said, with a twisted smile. He was slumped in his chair, the cigar forgotten. 'You should have followed your instincts and got rid of him; the writing was on the wall when Strachan began raising objections and stormed out of the last meeting. Events will prove you were also wrong to pin a badge on Zac Hunter – as I've already pointed out – because clearly he's the catalyst. But there's no sense in mopping up spilt milk. What we do now is make damn sure we see this through to a satisfactory conclusion.'

Jarrow had returned to his chair. His face was flushed. His eyes refused to meet Coburn's critical gaze.

'Nothing's changed,' he said huskily. 'With Leland out of the way and Rogers no use to man nor beast the opposition's down to just two – and one's an old man.'

'Not two.' The leather chair squeaked as Coburn shook his head. 'Two irate councillors, yes – but they're the least of our worries. Thanks to you there's a town marshal who last night was talking at great length to Lyne Barret. According to Yantze, he was gunned down, then rescued by a mystery man. Today he turns up, large as life. Alongside him you've got Quint – a man who's been in town five months and remains an enigma. Finally, there's the men lined up alongside Barret.'

'His foreman was drinking in Cobb's. We talked, as usual. He told me the drillers want no part in it. He wants no part of any violence, but he's willing to listen, and pass on information.'

'Forget the workers, I'm talking about Hollingsworth, Hamilton, Flint, and Earle. They've sunk a heap of cash into that company. They'll fight till they drop.'

For a few minutes there was silence. Coburn leaned forward to mash his cigar in the buffalo-hoof ashtray. Jarrow seemed to have shrunk into himself. His head was down and he was staring at his clasped hands.

'Hunter never did believe you had him over a barrel,'

Coburn mused aloud. 'You were a fool, and you acted without thinking.' He held up a hand as Jarrow made as if to protest. 'The point is, knowing he was free to go, Hunter hung around. There has to be a reason. Get over to the jail. Talk to him. Find out what he and Barret discussed, what Strachan and Cotter had to say.'

'Waste of time—'

'Maybe. But with you out of here, I've got time to think. One thing you did get right: it's drawing close to decision time. If Barret doesn't strike oil in the next couple of days. . . .'

'We move on him?'

Coburn shrugged. 'Maybe we do, maybe we don't, but the final decision will be mine—'

'Come on, Coburn, that's—'

'No, you've said enough, now get out there and do some work. But while you're out there, remember this: just like it was with Drake back in '58 and '59, just like those gunslingers Yantze and Levin – you, my good friend Jarrow, are working for me.'

In the sudden silence a furious Morgan Jarrow, bunched muscle jumping in his jaw, let his gaze drift to the heavy Indian club that rested on nails hammered into the wall behind Coburn's desk.

FIFTEEN

'D'you see that?'

Strachan and Cotter had just departed and were cutting across the square on the way back to their businesses. Hunter was standing on the plank walk outside the jail office. After taking his eyes away from his two departing visitors he'd been watching the clouds breaking up, the hot sun blazing through to begin drawing the moisture from the mud churned up across the square. But that was not what had caught his eye.

'That's Jake Rogers, the barber, over there by the bank and looking mighty worried,' Quint said, behind him. 'If you ask me, the only place that man could've been is Coburn's office.'

'Strachan seems to be thinking along similar lines. Soon as he spotted Rogers he looked back, signalled to me.'

'We know Rogers was the man who didn't raise his hand at that meeting, but what the hell's his game? And what can he do? He took so little from that talk he surely

108

had nothing to give to Coburn?'

'He had enough. I think he's put me on the spot, made my position a hell of a sight riskier than it was. Rogers knows Strachan and Cotter were planning to talk to me. It's possible he saw them coming here. *That's* the news he took to Coburn, and Coburn will warn Jarrow.'

For a few minutes the two men stood in the doorway watching the hustle and bustle of an early autumn morning in Nacogdoches. The plank walks on either side of Main Street and the square were now crowded with people strolling, conversing with acquaintances, or heading with purpose towards some business or other where they would make purchases, or be provided with a service. Strachan and Cotter, newspaper editor and hostler, were two who provided services that were frequently used. Leland, the gunsmith, had been another and, because of the lawlessness that was rife in the immense area that stretched west from the Mississippi all the way to the Pacific Ocean, he had always been in demand.

But not any more, Hunter thought. He watched absently as the mail coach clattered into the square, scattering riders and walkers as it took the diagonal route across to the bank. The driver jumped down. He walked forward several paces through the drying mud to check the lathered team of horses, then hopped into the coach to emerge seconds later with a package which he carried into the building. His movements brought back sharply to Hunter the violence that had exploded inside that same building little more than twenty-four hours ago and, with a sour taste in his mouth, he turned away and went back into the office.

Quint came back in more slowly, watching Hunter.

'Remember I made that bed up for you in the cell?' he said. 'I wonder if you'll use it tonight?'

'Never can tell,' Hunter said.

'Or are you off out of town again?' He waited. 'You've not said much about your visit to the drillings; what happened out there?'

Hunter chose to ignore both questions, and come back with one of his own. He was finding it difficult to break through to the real Quint, to find out why the man had drifted into Nacogdoches, a small town, and settled into a job that made him little more than a poorly paid lackey. In the immediate aftermath of the violence in the bank he'd had the appearance of a man with little imagination who was simply taking his cues from Morgan Jarrow. Later Hunter had looked more closely and, perhaps catching the deputy in an unguarded moment, had seen the intelligence in his eyes. Too much intelligence, Hunter thought now, for him to achieve fulfilment as deputy marshal of a small town.

'When Strachan and Cotter were in here earlier, you seemed keen to stress you were backing them – even though I was undecided then, and remain that way. Why is that? Morgan Jarrow gave you your job: why are you willing to side with men aiming to bring him down?'

Quint's gaze was shrewd. 'You came back at me with a question, so I'll do the same: Morgan Jarrow's done you no favours at all, so why are you sitting on the fence, refusing to allow you'll back Strachan and Cotter?'

But I'm not sitting on the fence, Hunter thought; my mind's made up. All I'm doing is letting Quint believe that's what I'm doing. And why? Because I'm not sure of the man – and in answer to his question about Strachan and Cotter, that's the line I'll take.

'Four men were in Cobb's back room. One's dead. One refused to count himself in when there was a show of hands. With that much doubt or uncertainty in a group, a man would be a fool to take sides—'

He broke off as the door was pushed open and the driver of the mail coach stepped in off the plank walk. He was short, bow-legged, dressed in dusty range clothes and with the front of his Stetson pressed back flat against the hat's crown. He nodded brightly at Hunter and tossed him a package.

'More work for you,' he said, as Hunter caught it. 'Bunch of dodgers offerin' rewards for the capture of convicts on the run, owlhoots runnin' wild, and dang me if there ain't a killer on the loose who—'

He was on his way out, still talking, when he was almost bowled over by a man dressed in a dark suit and pearl-grey sombrero who barged past him and into the office. He was breathing hard. His eyes blazed with excitement, his face was flushed and glistening.

'Tyne Coburn's dead,' he blurted. 'I've damn near run all the way from his office, and with my heart that's just asking for trouble. But Coburn's my lawyer, goddammit. I'm in business and I need his acumen – and now he's dead.'

'Slow down,' Hunter said quietly, as the newcomer began pacing up and down, his wild eyes flashing here and there, never settling. 'You walked into Coburn's office – and what happened, what did you find there?'

'The man's been beaten to death. There's blood everywhere, splashed on the desk, the walls. . . .'

He trailed off, and it was as if his recollections of the scene he was describing were too much for him. The colour left his face. His hand flapped, found the back of a chair, and it scraped across the floor as he dragged it towards him and slumped into it.

'Coburn kept . . . mementos,' he said distantly. 'One was some kind of heavy club, something an Injun'd use, rawhide wrapped around the grip, single eagle feather. . . .' He shook his head, stared at Hunter. 'That's what his killer used. It's on the desk. You'd best get over there. I left the door open when I ran, left it wide open with the body there for all to see.'

When Hunter left Quint he was talking to the wilting businessman who had removed his expensive grey hat and was using it to fan his face. Hunter gave him a reassuring pat on the shoulder, then thudded across the plank walk, jogged through the gluey mud of the square and into the high street. There were no horses tethered outside Coburn's office. When he turned into the still-open doorway, the office was in deep shadow, and empty but for the unmistakable smell of death. Carefully he closed the door behind him, leaned his back against it and surveyed a scene of horror.

Tyne Coburn was on his back, sprawled on the floor in front of the desk with his arms out-flung, hands curled. His face was an unrecognizable mass of bone and blood.

Around him the room had been demolished. Smashed glass from a tall cabinet lay glittering on the floor. The buffalo-hoof ashtray and pretty well everything else that had been on the desk had been swept away and was scattered across the rugs.

Streaks of blood glistened on the desk's polished surface. And, just as the shocked businessman had reported, the Indian club that had been used to commit murder had been placed there by the killer.

Who did this, Hunter wondered as he swallowed the bile rising in his throat? At first the only names he could come up with were Yantze and Levin; could only suppose that there had been a fracas of some kind that had split the group and left Coburn dead.

Then, in a flash, he was back in the bright sunlight shining on the doorway of the jail office, squinting across the square at the scurrying figure of Jake Rogers. Bart Strachan was frantically signalling to him. Quint was whispering in his ear: '*If you ask me, the only place that man could've been is Coburn's office.*'

So be it, Hunter thought.

He stepped away from the door, careful to keep his boots out of the sticky pools of blood, and looked behind him. The key was on the inside of the door, in the lock. As the thought flashed through his mind that if Coburn had made better use of it he might still be alive, he was already removing it. He stepped out into the street, slammed and locked the door, then made his way to the square.

Back in the jail office, there was no sign of Quint.

113

Hunter placed Coburn's key out of sight in a drawer then looked towards the stove. The coffee pot was gently bubbling. He crossed to it, splashed hot java into a tin cup, saw that there was the faintest of tremors in his fingers. Comparing that sign of weakness with Strachan's estimation of him as a force to be reckoned with, he sat behind the desk, pulled open another drawer and extracted a bottle. Willing his hand to be steady, he unscrewed the top from the bottle and splashed a stiff measure of whiskey into the cup.

When he sat back, holding the cup in both hands and sipping the doubly strong liquid that now packed the kick of a mule, his wandering gaze alighted on the package that had arrived with the mail coach. For a few moments he stared at it, recalling the coach driver's words, wondering if he could be bothered to open it; wondering what he was going to say to Jake Morgan; wondering, more than anything else, how the hell he'd ended up sitting in a small-town jail with a marshal's badge pinned to his vest and a duty to uphold the law.

Then he sighed and reached for the package.

He put down the cup, tore open the tough paper and let the package's contents spill onto the desk. Mostly wanted dodgers, several official letters from the Texas State authorities that Hunter glanced at then put to one side, more advertisements for everything from miracle cures for almost every ailment to Colt's latest single-action belt pistols.

What caught Hunter's eye was a single sheet of crisp paper. With quickening pulse, he read:

Reward

A substantial reward will be paid to anyone providing information leading to the arrest of the person or persons responsible for the brutal murder of Texas Ranger Teddy Anderson. Anderson's body was discovered in scrub to the north-west of Waco in May of this year. He had been shot in the back of the head. Information can be handed in to any. . . .

Hunter stopped reading and slapped the reward notice on the desk. He sat back, unaware that hot coffee had spilt over the back of his hand. So disturbed had he been when he walked in that he had left the office door wide open – it had been open anyway, left that way by Quint when he made a hurried departure. Now he was looking straight out across the sunlit square, but what he was seeing was not that rutted area of drying mud and beyond it the bank buildings. Instead he was once again standing in the office with a man who was holding in his cupped hand the badge of the Texas Rangers and telling Hunter, with a cold look in his eyes, that he wanted what Hunter had seen kept very quiet indeed.

Only now, with the arrival of the mail coach, did Hunter understand why.

SIXTEEN

The two heavily armed men keen-eyed trapper Gregor McCrae had spotted on one of his hunting trips were sitting on logs close to their fire but well away from the still dripping cottonwoods when Quint rode into their encampment on the banks of the winding creek. The wet grass sloping down to the water sparkled, but the sun that had burst through the breaking clouds was quickly lifting surface moisture that now hung as a thin mist only slowly being dispersed by the gentle breeze.

Norris and Shafton had never volunteered any first names, and Quint had obliged by withholding his. The three men had come together when Quint, wanted for murder, had been picked up trying to cross the Brazos and was on his way to the Waco jail in the custody of Teddy Anderson. The exhausted Texas Ranger had called a halt when he spotted the slender wisp of white smoke from the camp-fire rising into searing blue skies. His mistake had been in accepting the offer of coffee and vittles and talking too openly to Norris and Shafton. Worn out by constant vigilance in oppressive heat, he

116

had relaxed his guard. While Norris and Shafton held the ranger in conversation, Quint had worked his way behind him with the knife Shafton had been using to slice beef.

Now Quint rode into their camp without haste, resigned to the fact that the mail coach-driver's words and the contents of the package he'd placed on Zac Hunter's desk had well and truly cooked his goose. He had been waiting impatiently for the mail package, knew from constant monitoring of weekly deliveries that the reward notice was overdue, and now he could take a well-earned breather because roles had been reversed. Nacogdoches was out of bounds to him. Any news of Lyne Taliaferro Barret's progress out at the Skillern tract drillings would be picked up by Norris and Shafton, who were unknown in the town.

Unsurprisingly, the two men were elated after months spent out in the wild.

'Had to come,' Shafton said, when he heard the news. 'Only thing surprises me is that as deputy you couldn't have taken that reward notice and screwed it up before Hunter got to sniffing at it.'

'Not worth the effort,' Quint said, stripping the rig from his horse and dumping it up against the bole of one of the cottonwoods. 'Besides, things are moving so fast a couple of fresh faces in town will either go unnoticed, or make a welcome change. McCrae's dead, Frank Leland's dead – now Coburn's gone, battered to death by Jake Rogers.'

'Coburn?' Norris said. He was a blocky man with red hair and a pale skin. 'If the lawyer man's dead, does that make it easier for us?'

'We got wind of Barret's hunt for oil six months ago,' Quint said, settling down across the fire from the two gunmen, tilting his hat down to keep the sun from his eyes. 'For a full legal takeover of Barret's operation – before or after an oil strike, and assuming he'd be willing to sell – a heap of cash would be needed. That always counted us out, and for an armed takeover at any time three men were never going to give us enough fire power. I came up with the notion of joining forces with someone in the same boat – with oil promising a fortune to anyone involved, I knew the vultures would be circling. So I moved into Nacogdoches to sniff the air, test the water. That led me to Morgan Jarrow.' He grinned. 'Or maybe he led me to him, took me on without considering the consequences.'

'Which brings me back to my question,' Norris said, dragging the makings from his pocket and absently hefting the tobacco sack in his palm. 'You saw an opportunity, a way in for us: Jarrow was planning an armed takeover of Melrose Oil, but he was relying too much on Yantze and Levin. OK, Coburn and Jarrow would have added some weight, but now Coburn's gone. Jarrow's down to three men, same as us. So my question is, will he go ahead, move in on Barret – or figure the game's up, back off and walk away?'

'He won't walk away,' Quint said. 'He's been dreaming of this since Drake back in '59. And, to answer your question, Coburn's death makes it easier for us. You've just made the point: with the lawyer gone, his force is reduced by a quarter. Jarrow needs us now more than ever.'

'But he doesn't know that yet, does he? He must be worried about his weakness, but he doesn't know me and Norris are out here, doesn't know we've been in this with you for more'n five months. So he's going to be nervous, wondering when to make his move, wondering if he's going to make that move and get wiped out.'

That was Shafton again, a gaunt man with bony wrists and big hands. He was looking steadily at Quint as he made those points, his hands busy with a steel rod and cotton patch he was using to clean the barrel of his Remington New Model Army .44 revolver.

'A weak man would fold under the pressure,' Norris said. 'You always reckoned Jarrow's weak.'

'Coburn was a Confederate Army deserter,' Quint said, and he grinned. 'Morgan Jarrow doesn't have that much integrity, or guts.'

'Right. So when he begins to buckle, we move in and make him an offer.'

'When the time's right,' Quint said, nodding. He caught the tobacco sack Norris tossed across the fire, and grinned again. 'Who knows, if Jarrow's impetuosity overcomes his natural cowardice, the right time for us could well be when the bullets begin to fly.'

SEVENTEEN

Realizing that Quint had skedaddled and was unlikely to return, Hunter took to pacing the office with his cup of fiery coffee. Mentally, he was scratching his head. Quint was an enigma turned into a nightmare, and Hunter had to face the possibility that the deputy had been hanging around hoping to pick up some crumbs if Jarrow succeeded in ousting Lyne Barret. If so, then he'd failed. That he was a killer was neither here nor there, because he'd hightailed and must be dealt with at another time, by other men. Of more importance was the killer still in town but, to get to Jake Rogers, Hunter needed somebody to mind the office.

He downed the last of his drink, scrawled BACK IN AN HOUR on a square of cardboard and used twine to hang it on the handle when he strode out and locked the door. A hurried walk up the street took him across to the hardware store where he asked Tobin, the proprietor, to get a message to his son that he was needed at the jail.

Then Hunter walked back down the street to the barber's shop.

A man was walking out, traces of soap lining his pink jaw. Hunter stepped to one side, then walked in. Rogers was on his own, washing a razor in a tin bowl. He looked over his shoulder.

'Heard about Coburn,' he said. 'Bad thing. First Levin. Now this.'

He shook the razor dry, snapped it shut and walked away from the bowl.

'You visited Coburn this morning.'

The flat statement shook Rogers. His brow furrowed. He took his lower lip between his teeth, thought for a moment then shook his head.

'No; I admit I was down that way—'

'You were seen entering and leaving the office,' Hunter said, lying easily. 'I'd say you were the last man to see Coburn alive.'

'And you'd be wrong.' Rogers shook his head furiously, suddenly more sure of himself. 'The two of them were there, Coburn and Jarrow. They were there when I got there, still there when I left.'

'I've only your word for that.'

'The witnesses who saw me must have seen Jarrow.'

'Maybe they were there, but only one was alive. You and Jarrow were in this together. You murdered Coburn, left separately – you first.' He looked at the tin bowl of soapy water. 'Whoever beat Coburn with an Indian club would have blood on his hands. Is that why you hurried back here?'

In the tense silence Hunter drifted forward, bent his knees to look in a cracked and misted mirror, adjusted his hat.

121

'Or maybe you're right, Rogers. Maybe Coburn was alive when you walked out. But what about Jarrow? Was he arguing with Coburn?'

He could see Rogers' reflection. The man was licking his lips. Suddenly aware of the razor in the hand of a man who could be a killer, Hunter swung round.

'Were they arguing, exchanging harsh words, threats?'

'No.'

'Why did you go there?'

'I—'

'There was a show of hands in Cobb's back room. You kept yours in your pockets. That puts you on the fence, or favouring the other side. If you saw Strachan and Cotter in my office, you might have thought that information worth passing on to Jarrow. Is that why you went there?'

'If I did,' Rogers said, 'it was for the good of the town. Whatever I do, it will be for the good of the town. Jarrow is a good man. I'm backing him all the way.'

'A good man who feels the need to have hired gunslingers on his payroll.'

Rogers smiled slyly. 'Not a bad idea if there's a killer on the loose.'

'What if he intends to use them to drive Barret off the drillings?'

'He'll do what's right for the town,' Rogers said stubbornly. '*I'll* do what's right for the town.'

Hunter snapped his fingers impatiently.

'Where can I find Jarrow?'

'He sleeps in the rooming-house. During the day, I've no idea.'

Jaw tight, Hunter swung on his heel and walked out of the shop. For several moments he stood on the plank walk, tasting the dust being lifted from the now dry street by the breeze, feeling the heat of the afternoon sun on his face. He looked to his left to the gunsmith's premises where Frank Leland had been knifed, then down the street to the square where two men had gunned down Marshal Danny McCrae in the bank. Then had themselves been gunned down, Hunter reflected bitterly. Now another man had been beaten to death. And all for what? For oil – yet no oil had been found, perhaps would never be found. And he, Hunter realized, was now a man alone, looked up to with expectation by two men trying their damnedest to put back the clock, to return Nacogdoches to a more settled recent past.

Too much to expect of him, he admitted – and even as the thought entered his head he saw the unmistakable figure of Gregor McCrae riding down the street and drawing to a halt in front of Cobb's Old Colonial saloon.

'Something's telling me this whole shebang's about to rattle off the rails,' Hunter said, 'and, as of now, I don't know what I can do to prevent it happening.'

'If you can't see a way to stop it, son, wait until the fireworks start. I've always found bullets buzzing like hornets around the ears work wonders for a man's sluggish thought processes.'

Gregor McCrae spoke with firm conviction and, from his own Civil War experiences, Hunter knew he was right. Besides, putting it bluntly, waiting for the fun to start was the only damn thing he *could* do.

He'd been sitting with McCrae at a table in Cobb's place for a considerable time. Darkness had descended over Nacogdoches, the oil lamps were casting their glow over Main Street and the square, and the saloon was beginning to fill up with thirsty cowboys, drifters, and businessmen who had locked up for the day and walked wearily up the street to wash the dust from dry throats.

In the time they had been sitting there, Hunter had brought McCrae up to date with all that had been happening in the town. The trapper had listened intently, and had quickly come around to Hunter's point of view. Sure, it had been bad enough when there was the pure, absolute certainty that Morgan Jarrow was going after Lyne Barret's oil, he'd agreed. But with the added complications of Strachan and his dwindling band, the transformation of Quint from deputy town marshal and Texas Ranger to a cold-blooded killer – well, yes, there was plenty there to send a man into some deep cogitating.

'On top of that,' Hunter added, 'Morgan Jarrow seems to have disappeared along with Yantze and Levin.'

'He won't make a move until Barret gets lucky,' McCrae said. 'Which reinforces my conviction that we sit tight.'

'We?'

The big trapper, a glass in his hand as he teetered his chair on two legs, was grinning happily.

'I've seen you in action, son. You need somebody to hold your hand, point out the low branches, tell you when to duck your head.'

Then the chair's legs were gently lowered to the

sawdust and he reached across the table to clamp his big hand on Hunter's wrist.

'Don't make the mistake of looking over your shoulder too sudden,' he said, 'but the two bad eggs who've just walked in look awful like the fellows I saw camped on the creek a ways west of the Skillern.'

'Seen them in town before?'

'Like I said, I get to town once a month for provisions and a shave. I wouldn't say that was often enough to judge if they're regular visitors.'

'And as I rode into Nacogdoches for the first time a couple of days ago, I'm not much help.'

Hunter thought for a moment, hit on what seemed like inspiration, then grimaced at the odds against his being right.

'Something?'

'Quint leaves town in a hurry, hours later two strangers walk into Cobb's place. Coincidence?'

McCrae pursed his lips, still carefully watching the newcomers.

'If they were two ordinary fellows minding their own business, I'd say yes. But I told you I watch people, and those two mean characters, eyes looking every which way, Colt revolvers with shiny butts sitting loose in tied-down holsters – no, son, coincidence is not the word I'd choose.'

'But you never saw Quint out there at their camp?'

'Nope.'

'Then his link with them doesn't get beyond a bright idea?'

'Not yet it don't – but I always did put a lot of trust in hunches.'

He got up and wandered across to the bar, watched by the big saloonist, Cobb. Now Hunter was able to turn without it looking too obvious, and at once his gaze homed in on the two men who were already at the bar ordering drinks. Mean was right. He put them alongside Yantze and Levin in the degree of menace that emanated from them so strongly that others at the bar were giving them plenty of elbow room.

McCrae wasn't impressed. He pushed in close enough to the taller of the two to rub hard against his shoulder. Both men turned their heads to look at him. Hunter saw them take in the buckskin jacket, the moccasin-soft boots, the Bowie knife, and swiftly dismiss him as a clumsy, no-account backwoodsman not worthy of their attention.

Then, as the door again banged open, he tore his gaze from them and saw Lyne Barret and John Flint walking in. The oil chief saw him at once. He touched Flint's arm, nodded towards Hunter then veered away from his companion and came over to the table.

'We're so close I'm getting goose bumps,' he said, suppressed excitement glowing in his eyes as he dragged out a chair. 'Down to more than ninety feet through hard rock, as of this morning, and there's some mighty strange rumblings coming up that pipe.'

'If you strike, is there any way you can keep the news under your hats?'

'Not a chance. Even if we could, we wouldn't. Ben Hollingsworth's been called home and, as we haven't heard from Charlie Hamilton and Johnnie Earle, I'm in town again tomorrow talking to the bank. If we've struck oil, I'm forced to tell. Good news will practically guarantee finance.'

He looked up as John Flint and McCrae appeared at the table carrying fresh drinks. Both Flint and Barret seemed comfortable in the trapper's presence, and suddenly Hunter wondered what the big backwoodsman had been holding back.

Flint, his jaw still stubborn, seemed to have relaxed his attitude towards Hunter now that the attempted bushwhacking had separated the marshal from Jarrow, and he nodded in a friendly way as he tasted his drink. McCrae was watching all of this with a faint smile as he sat down.

Amused – or secretive, Hunter wondered.

He half-turned from the table, let his gaze drift. The two gunmen had their backs to the bar, elbows resting. They were trying hard to give the impression that they were casually looking over the whole room, but their eyes strayed too often towards the table where the four men were sitting, and Hunter felt a surge of excitement.

If his hunch was right, they were with Quint. But what if he was wrong? Jarrow, too, appeared to have left town suddenly. What if these men were his? Did that make Lyne Barret's chances better or worse?

He was suddenly aware that under the growing volume of noise in the saloon as strong drink was consumed, voices were raised, and frequent bursts of laughter became strong enough to bring dust from trembling beams drifting down through the glow of hanging oil lamps, the three men at the table were bent forward over their drinks and talking earnestly.

Barret was the first to notice that Hunter had come out of his reverie. He stopped, and first Flint then Gregor McCrae turned their gaze towards the marshal. Again that half-smile flickered around the backwoodsman's lips. He shook his head.

'I guess I wasn't too straight with you, son.'

'You either were or you weren't. There's no halfway.'

'But the good intentions were there, and everything worked out a treat. You see, I've known these fellows since they first approached Lucy Skillern back in '59 and got themselves a lease.' He chuckled, and looked warmly at Barret and Flint. 'Difficult not to get to know them, seeing as in a way they were on my land.'

'You saying you've got shares?'

'Some. But that's only right seeing as I'm what you might call their eyes and ears. And yours too, son. That was no accident, me arriving in the nick of time to save your bacon. Lyne sent me out after you.'

'Why?'

'There was a chance you were lying through your teeth. If you linked up with that Yantze fellow who was hanging around, then that would've been proof that you were working with Jarrow.'

For a moment Hunter was furious. Then he saw the good sense in Barret's extreme caution that had sent McCrae after him, and he nodded his grudging acknowledgement to the oilman.

'Well, as I didn't ride back into town with Yantze—'

'As it happens, that was an impossibility,' McCrae interrupted. 'Another way I was a mite sparing with the truth was in not letting on I recognized the man who tried to knock you out of the saddle.' He paused, watching Hunter. 'Yantze was nowhere to be seen. The man who took those shots at you wasn't Yantze, it was Deputy Marshal Quint.'

And, before the shock of that startling revelation had been fully absorbed, Hunter heard the saloon doors bang open yet again and saw Yantze and Levin walk in and make for the bar.

'I'm looking for Morgan Jarrow,' Hunter said, closing in on the two men.

Yantze flicked a glance at Levin, a mocking smile curling his lips beneath the drooping moustache.

'The man says he's looking for Jarrow,' he said in the hoarse voice Hunter remembered from Coburn's office. 'D'you see him in here, Lev?'

Levin, dark-bearded and sardonic, played along. He turned theatrically from the bar to survey the crowded room, wide-eyed, then shook his head.

'Nope,' he said, amusement in his black eyes. 'Can't see no sign of him.'

'That's not funny, it's pathetic,' Hunter said scathingly. 'You both work for him, you must know where I can find him.'

'Maybe we do, maybe we don't,' Yantze said. 'And maybe me deciding how much to tell you depends on what you want with Jarrow.'

Hunter shook his head impatiently.

'Forget Jarrow. You'll do. I've got a warning for him. You can pass it on. Tell your boss that any attempted takeover of Barret's oil operations is against the law. If necessary, force will be used to press home that point.'

'Talks fancy, don't he?' Yantze said to Levin. 'Him with his *attempted takeovers* and *pressin' home points*.' Then he cocked one eyebrow at Hunter. 'Force, you say? I take it that means you with that worthless tin badge, and those three losers over there?' He jerked his head towards the table where Hunter had been sitting with McCrae and the oilmen.

'It does. Those three, plus whoever and however many it takes.'

'There ain't no more,' Yantze jeered. 'This town's filled with spineless yeller-bellies; they're what you've got: they're *all* you've got.'

'Don't count on it,' Hunter said flatly.

He saw something flicker in Yantze's pale eyes. Doubt? The first realization that there were undercurrents of activity in the town that had escaped Jarrow's notice? Or something else? Could it be that Yantze knew that Jarrow, like the great British Duke, Wellington, was holding some of his forces in reserve on the other side of a nearby ridge? But no, surely not, for weren't the other two gunmen at the bar Quint's men?

'What about those fellows over there?' Hunter said thoughtfully, gesturing towards the two gunmen still drinking at the other end of the bar. 'They Jarrow's men?'

'Anyone with sense is a Jarrow man,' Yantze said with a smirk, 'but if you want to know for sure, go ask them.'

With that he turned his back on Hunter, picked up his drink and began talking to Levin.

It occurred to Hunter as he drifted away from the two

gunmen and saw the massive figure of Cobb walking along the other side of the bar with his face glistening and beetling brows in their permanent position of brooding gloom that saloonists, by the nature of their job, picked up most of the gossip circulating in a town. Was he worth talking to? Would he know the two men he was even now addressing?

Almost certainly, Hunter thought but, even as he hesitated, he knew that the time for talk had passed. The two gunmen who could be Quint's, could be Jarrow's, nodded to Cobb, then drank up and left the saloon. At the same time Hunter saw Barret and Flint push back from the table, and he realized they too were leaving. He hurried over to them, but saw at once that the same position had been reached: the talking was all done. Barret's mind was clearly back at the Skillern tract and he was unable to keep the excitement out of his eyes and his manner as he contemplated the likelihood of an imminent oil strike. Flint, too, was finding it hard to keep still; it was as if the grind of the big drill and the throb of the steam engine as it powered the auger down through solid rock were always present in his brain, as much a part of him as his pulse. He planted his hat on his head, waited for Barret to shake hands with Hunter, then nodded to the marshal and both men left the saloon.

As Hunter sat down, he heard the whinny of a horse, the rattle of hoofs receding up Main Street then swiftly fading as the two oilmen left town. He looked at McCrae, and shook his head.

'No luck with Yantze and his pard. If they know where Jarrow is, they're not saying. And I'm no closer to knowing if the other two are Quint's men.'

'Rest easy. You had it right. I heard them talking about Quint when I was at the bar. For now, Barret knows everyone's holding their breath while they wait for that oil to come gushing from the earth – and I do mean everyone: oilmen, villains with fast guns, chancers waiting to move in when the news hits town. But it's getting late. Nothing's going to happen tonight. I'm off home to get a good night's sleep, and I suggest you do the same—'

He broke off as he saw Levin making his way towards the street door, Yantze coming towards the table. The grey, scarred gunman was looking at Hunter.

'Hey now, Marshal, I just recalled where Jarrow said he was going,' he said. 'He heard about Hollingsworth riding out, and got advance word that Barret and Flint would be in town tonight. That gave him his chance – but how'd it happen? Well, where he is now is out there at the Skillern talking to a friend of his who's on the drilling gang. Putting it another way, Jarrow's got a powerful insider so everything done or said out there at the drillings gets back to him. He knows for sure they're going to strike oil within the next few hours. When they do, Lyne Barret is going to get one hell of a surprise.'

EIGHTEEN

12 September, 1866

Hunter had bidden goodnight to Gregor McCrae outside Cobb's Old Colonial, then walked down the hill and across the moonlit square to spend his first night in the jail-cell bed prepared for him by Quint. Before settling down on the hard cot, he had told the young night man, Scott Tobin, to wake him at once if there was hot news from the Skillern tract.

His sleep was undisturbed. He awoke to a day of sunshine and clear blue skies, and after breakfast at the café he had stepped out onto the plank walk and leaned against the already warming wall of the building to relax and watch Nacogdoches' day begin.

But what would the day bring, he wondered, as Rogers hurried by on the way to his shop, his eyes averted? Would the barber's former friend, Strachan, play any part in the momentous events that even now seemed to be causing the hot air to crackle with unseen tension? Would the old-timer, Cotter, who had poked his head out of the livery barn higher up the street and lifted his hand to Hunter? Across the square the bank's doors banged open and the man called Soames glanced across towards him. Whatever happened, Barret would be walking through that door today, Hunter remembered, cap in hand. But when he arrived, would he be the man to bring the good news of the oil strike? Or was that news even now being brought into town by a man on a fast horse? And if it was, had Jarrow been apprised of it much earlier by his contact out there in the drilling team? Was he even now launching an attack, his two gunmen throwing down a withering fire on the drillings using their rifles from a distance before riding in to finish the job with their six-guns? And what of Quint, and the two men McCrae had overhead discussing the man with the ranger's badge? Were they with Jarrow, against him? Or neither, but intent on a lone bid to line their own pockets?

Hunter sighed. It was all too complicated. A bank robbery gave the protagonists instant reward – he smiled crookedly at the irony of that thought – but what reward could be gained by any crooked outsider from a venture that by its nature produced profit over a period of time?

Don't know, Hunter thought; don't know any of it, and have no way of finding out in a hurry, which is what was needed if he was to get to the bottom of things in the short time available.

Still no further ahead with his thinking than he had been when he left the café, Hunter set off down the street and along the side of the square to the jail office. Scott Tobin the tow-headed young night man was dozing behind the desk. Hunter sent him on his way, then tossed his hat onto the peg and settled down behind the desk with the rest of the paperwork from the mail package spread before him.

Like it or not, he thought, he was town marshal, and so for the rest of the morning he got on with the job, only sending the occasional glance through the wide open door and across the sunlit square to the bank. Yet by the time midday approached and passed, even those glances had been enough to tell him that Lyne Barret hadn't made it into town – and it was with the conviction that something was badly wrong that Hunter stood up, stretched and went out onto the plank walk.

Had the illegal takeover of Barret's drilling operations taken place, without any word of it reaching the town? Squinting anxiously in the direction of Main Street, he had to admit that was more than a possibility. The Skillern tract was pushing thirteen miles to the east. Barret could have struck oil during the night. Jarrow could have got wind of it – could have been close by in the woods, watching for just such a happening, waiting for word from his contact – and at dawn moved in with Yantze and Levin and their blazing guns. It could all be over, the oilmen gunned down, a triumphant Jarrow sitting in the cabin with his feet up on Barret's desk.

And then there was Quint.

Hunter drew a breath, unable to shed the dark thoughts that were painting every possible situation in the blackest of colours. Yet just when the tension had settled into a dull ache behind his eyes and he'd decided the only way to avoid driving himself crazy was to set off for Cotter's barn, collect his horse and ride out to the tract, two things happened that stopped him in his tracks.

Firstly, the two men he was convinced were Quint's gunslingers came ambling down the plank walk from the rooming house, looked across towards the jail, then turned into the café.

Then, as the door banged shut behind them and Hunter caught the faint tinkle of the premises' bell, Lyne Barret came riding down the street on a dusty grey mare. He cantered across the square, swung down and tied the horse to the rail. Without a backward glance, he walked into the bank.

Glory be, Hunter thought, and a grin split his face. Quint's two gunslingers were still in town. Barret was going about his business, and he surely wouldn't be doing that if there was trouble at the diggings. That meant Jarrow hadn't yet made his move. If he hadn't, then—

A sound broke into his thoughts.

As he stepped away from the wall the sound clarified and became the swelling drum of hoofbeats entering the town. He turned to watch as a horseman appeared at the end of Main Street and dragged his plume of dust all the way into the square where he threw himself from the saddle.

'Oil strike!' he yelled, boots planted in the dust, his hand white-knuckled on the saddle-horn as he looked around him at the passers-by who everywhere had stopped to stare. 'Lyne Barret's crew's just struck oil at the Skillern tract. Every man jack out there's black and shiny with the stuff, dancing Irish jigs and laughing fit to bust.'

Then everyone in the square seemed to be shouting at once. The door to the bank opened and Lyne Barret charged out. He leaped down from the plank walk, ran to the horseman and grabbed his arm. Hasty words were exchanged. Then, with a piercing yell of delight, Barret ripped off his hat and sent it spinning high into the air. There was a swelling roar of approval from onlookers. Quickly a crowd gathered around Barret, pressing in close, every man there wanting to shake his hand, pound him on the back.

The excitement was infectious. Hunter found himself grinning like a fool, felt the worry that had been eating at him like a canker swept away by a veritable tide of positive emotions that left no room for doubts or fears. It seemed that the entire population of Nacogdoches was converging on the square, every man, woman and child wanting to be part of the excitement.

All except two.

Movement up the street tore Hunter's eyes away from the tumult, from the mass of humanity surrounding Lyne Barret. Quint's men had left the café. As Hunter watched, they hurried up the street to Cotter's livery barn and disappeared inside. Almost immediately they reappeared, on horseback, and rode hard up the street towards the outskirts of town.

Got the news they've been waiting for, Hunter thought, again tight-lipped, and with a shake of his head he went into the office. Engulfed by excitement of a different kind, controlling it with an effort, he unhurriedly took down his gun-belt from its peg and buckled it about his waist. Then, thinking of the men he was to ride with, he unlocked the rack of guns.

NINETEEN

Excitement was still buzzing through the town of Nacogdoches when, as dusk drew its curtains over the land, Zac Hunter rode out with Lyne Barret, Bart Strachan and Sol Cotter. All four men were armed to the teeth. Both the newspaper editor and the old hostler had their own weapons. Luckily they were .44 calibre pistols and rifles: Hunter had found cartons of the correct ammunition in the jail office, and these he'd stuffed into his saddle-bags.

It was with a sense of unreality that the riders put the town behind them and pointed their horses towards the Skillern tract. Hunter's thoughts had lingered long on how Jarrow intended to handle a takeover. Now, as they clattered down the trail, he asked the other men for their opinion.

Sol Cotter was the first to answer. The old hostler said he had looked at the problem from every angle. There was only one way the takeover could be done, 'And even then' he said, 'it ain't going to work.'

'There's no cash until the well's up and running. But

our friend Barret here, he won't be forced into handing over control, not even at the point of a gun. That means the only way it'll work is if Jarrow removes him and his colleagues, in the only way that's guaranteed permanent.'

'With a bullet,' Strachan agreed, nodding. He turned in the saddle, glanced back at Barret who was a few yards behind. 'First, though, he's got to get onto the site, and even with Yantze and Levin that could prove difficult.'

'I spoke to both of you yesterday in the office,' Hunter said to Strachan and Cotter. 'Quint was there, and you'll remember he appeared to be with us. Things have changed. Paperwork's come in that points to him having murdered a Texas Ranger earlier this year. He left town in a hurry.' He hesitated. 'A trapper I know spotted two men camped some way to the west. From what he overheard last night, I think they're Quint's men.'

'You're talking about McCrae,' Lyne Barret said. 'Yeah, he told me about those two.'

Strachan was frowning. 'McCrae? Is there a connection?'

'His name's Gregor. He's the late Marshal Danny McCrae's brother.'

'I had dealings with those two fellers you're talking about,' Cotter growled. 'They'd stabled their horses. This afternoon when the whole town was going crazy they collected 'em, then refused to pay the going rate.'

'I was watching,' Hunter said. 'They rode out of your barn soon after that rider came down the street to announce the strike. By now, Quint will know all about it.'

140

Barret was frowning. 'You saying Quint and those two men are also after the oil?'

'I'd say so. If he is, your problems have doubled.'

Then he cast a glance at Cotter, eased the big bay off the trail and reined in. Caught by surprise, the others wheeled abruptly, puffs of dust spurting from beneath their horses' hoofs, then joined Hunter on the fringe of the trees.

'Trouble?' old Cotter said.

'You said something, and it almost went by me without touching the sides. I asked how Jarrow would work the takeover. You made a suggestion, but the bit at the end's come back to puzzle me: you said whatever he did, it wouldn't work. What's that mean?'

'Jarrow or Quint, take your pick,' Cotter said, doffing his hat and running a calloused hand across the glistening brown skin of his bald head. 'Both greedy men, both looking to make a fast buck, and both way out of their depth. If there's a gunfight there's two ways it can end, and both ways the owlhoots come out losers.'

'If they lose the battle for the tract they wind up dead or in the state pen,' Strachan said, catching on but not understanding. 'But if they win, they control the drillings. Sure, they won't get rich quick, but that doesn't make them losers.'

'They won't get rich, ever,' Lyne Barret said with finality. 'There's more to running a business than sitting back and watching the money roll in, and that's the point Cotter's making: if Jarrow or Quint blows me and my partners off the site, the business will fold within a month – oil or no oil.'

'They're fools,' Hunter said flatly. 'If I've worked it out right, Jarrow had the best of the ideas: take over Nacogdoches, control local government, then wait for the oilmen to make the town rich. But he wanted to get rich quick, couldn't sit back and listen to the clock ticking.' He looked across at Barret, relaxed in the saddle as he listened intently. 'One thing's for sure: if Jarrow and Quint do make a move, in their misguided attempt to avail themselves of a fortune, a lot of good men will die.'

The sun sank swiftly in the west. Darkness settled like a blanket and, by the time the four men drew near to the drillings on the Skillern tract, visibility was becoming a problem. Barret knew the trail like the back of his hand, and led the way with confidence. It was he who first spotted the soft glow of oil lamps filtering through the trees, and he held his hand high to slow down the following riders.

Hunter moved up alongside the oilman.

'Quint will have the news by now,' he said. 'Jarrow's not been seen since yesterday. If three of your partners are away from the site and the workers are not taking sides, Flint's on his own.'

'That was a risk I knew I was taking when I rode into town. I didn't expect the strike to come before I got back.'

'There's another thing,' Hunter said. 'Yantze spoke to me in Cobb's place. He told me Jarrow's got an insider at the drillings; one of your men's been feeding him with information.'

'If they have,' Barret said, 'that will be Cochran, the foreman.'

'You've suspected him?'

'Never. But of the six men working for us, he's the one who spends the most time in Nacogdoches. He's a coward. Talk's as far as it'll go.'

The four horses had their heads down, cropping the short grass under the shelter of the trees. Quiet settled over the men as each of them dug deep into his thoughts and experiences to see if anything in their past matched what lay ahead of them. A daunting and nigh-on impossible task, Hunter reflected, for whatever they came up with would be pure conjecture. None of them knew what they would be faced with when they reached the drillings where the new oil well was pumping the rich black mineral to the surface.

The way Hunter viewed it, the prospects looked bleak. Quint's men had left Nacogdoches with the hot news. Jarrow had been out of town since the previous day, but had a contact in the drilling team keeping him informed.

And John Flint, Hunter reminded himself, was out there on his own.

TWENTY

An early moon was a pale disc in cold, clear skies when the trail began to emerge from the trees and the skeletal shape of the derrick reared before them in the clearing. They had been riding in single file, spaced out. Barret was still leading. Once again he stopped, this time simply by drawing rein and turning his grey mare so that the way past him was blocked, then waiting until the other three men closed up and formed a tight group.

The lights he had spotted came from the low-slung cabin that a couple of days ago Hunter had figured was the drilling team's living quarters. Those lights were, Hunter judged, somewhat subdued, as if the men inside were keeping their heads down.

Back against the far timber, in the window of the other, smaller cabin that was the oilmen's headquarters, a single light glowed.

'Too quiet,' Barret said.

'Steam engine's shut down,' old Cotter said, with surprise. 'I was expectin' lights, thumping, pounding, the sound of thick liquid gushing.'

144

'We're not deep enough into the earth,' Barret said absently, his eyes busy. 'Whatever oil comes up will come up slow. In such circumstances it's enough to work during daylight hours. . . .'

He didn't finish what he was saying. All four men had been sniffing the damp, cooling air that carried the scents of pine trees and dank undergrowth, of the wood smoke that could be seen drifting from the long cabin's stone chimney and the richer smell of fresh earth and powdered rock. But in there, too, Barret had noticed another, sharper tang.

The oilman shivered.

'Gunpowder,' he said softly.

'I smell it,' Hunter said. 'We could be too late.'

'Never too late,' Barret said. 'If the drillings are taken, we take them back – and how many men are we looking at facing? Jarrow has—'

'Two.'

'Against four of us,' Strachan said. 'So what are we waiting for?'

'Not four, five,' a voice said. As if mounted on a ghostly steed, the big figure of Gregor McCrae astride his ragged mountain pony emerged with scarcely a crackle of twigs from the deep shadows of the forest.

Barret's intake of breath was audible.

'Greg,' he said huskily, 'welcome to the party. Can you tell us what's been going on here?'

'I heard two shots ring out, a lot of shouting, got here as fast as I could. It was already dusk. The drilling crew were back inside, the door shut. Those two Jarrow gunslingers were lugging John Flint from the small

145

cabin. His toes were dragging in the dust. They dumped him in that clutter under the derrick. He's there still.'

Barret was leaning on the saddle horn. His face was pale.

'How long ago?'

'Long enough for you fellows not to hear the shots. A half-hour?'

'You been watching since then?'

'No. I saw Jarrow talking to Yantze and Levin after they'd dumped Flint, then I did some scouting. Jarrow's too cocksure. There's a chance others are after the oil, and if they've heard the news they'll show up – right, Hunter?'

'Knowing Quint, I'd say it's certain.'

'So we move before that happens,' Sol Cotter said, and he looked at the burly trapper. 'I like the look of that big Sharps. Scare a man to death, that would.'

McCrae chuckled.

'Yeah, why don't I put a shot through the cabin window, see what happens?'

'Hold on,' Hunter said. 'I've spent the last five years with the Confederacy. If that experience taught me anything, it's that when men in a tight group come under fire, most of them are as good as dead. Before you use that Sharps, McCrae, we split up. Two men on the flanks: Strachan and Cotter. McCrae, you choose the best position for letting loose with that cannon. I'll stay here with Barret; in the woods on either side of the trail will put us under cover, but still able to observe.'

Sol Cotter was already wheeling his bronc to the left. Strachan did the same, in the opposite direction, then hauled back on the reins and addressed Hunter as his horse tossed its head, its teeth glistening white on the bit.

'Three possibilities come after McCrae's sent a big slug buzzing across their supper table,' he said, as the old hostler also held back, listening. 'One is they up and run – which ain't going to happen. Second is they sit tight – highly unlikely. Third is they come out with guns blazing, and that's damn near a certainty. So we need to decide now how we're going to play this.'

'You two on the flanks, get in a position with a good field of view, and hold your fire,' Hunter said. 'If Jarrow and his men come at us, I'll wait till they're close enough so every shot counts. When me and Barret begin shooting, that's your signal.' He did a swift calculation, then said, 'Thirty or forty yards should be far enough. McCrae will let loose a minute from now.'

Strachan nodded, then eased the reins and set his horse off at a walk along the edge of the woods, heading south. Cotter did the same, in a northerly direction. McCrae watched them go, then swung out of the saddle.

'Here's as good a place as any, for me,' he said. He led his horse onto the coarse grass and tethered it to a drooping branch. Then he dragged the Sharps from its saddle boot, walked forward a couple of paces and dropped to one knee.

Hunter looked at Barret.

'Ready for this?'

'Suddenly that goddamn oil's of secondary importance. John Flint's lying out there under the derrick. If he's alive, bleeding, he needs help fast. The sooner we get the sons of bitches who did that to him,

147

the quicker that happens.'

Face tight, he stepped out of the saddle and moved his horse off the trail to the left. Hunter followed suit, but went right. Then he called across to the kneeling trapper.

'The minute's up. Let's get this rolling, McCrae.'

Swiftly drawing his rifle, he melted into the woods. There was no sign of Barret, who had already taken cover. McCrae glanced around, checking on their location. Then he settled. He sat back on his heel, thrust the butt of the buffalo gun tight into his shoulder, and squeezed the trigger.

The detonation was like a bomb exploding. The muzzle flash lit up the overhanging trees, was reflected like a dull flash of lightning from the steam-engine's copper boiler. In that split second Hunter thought he saw a white face and a dark shape on the ground beneath the skeletal derrick, another metallic shine that could have come from a gun barrel almost hidden behind a stack of equipment. Then the big Sharps kicked high. The .50-.90 bullet hissed through the night air. Another split second later and the cabin window shattered. The sound of breaking glass came simultaneously with the clang of iron, then a high whine. This was followed instantly by the crunch of splintering shingle as the ricocheting slug tore through the roof.

Hunter had expected a violent reaction. In his planning he had visualized a rapid return of fire from rifles poked through the shattered window, or been prepared for the door bursting open and Jarrow and the

148

two gunslingers leaping forth and darting to the side with guns blazing.

Instead, he was appalled to hear the sudden fierce crackle of gunfire on both flanks. From the north there came the roar of a man in pain – abruptly choked off. To the south, the shooting simply stopped.

McCrae was up on his feet, reloading the Sharps. He backed towards Hunter. His eyes swept the clearing and the cabin for any sign of movement. Nothing stirred. As he neared Hunter, Barret came out of the shadows and into the moonlight. He crossed the trail at a run.

'They must have been waiting for them, for Cotter and Strachan,' he said. 'Maybe they saw them, maybe not—'

'I knew Coburn served with the Confederate forces,' Hunter said. 'Like a fool, I didn't credit Jarrow with the same experience. I guess he knew all about outflanking—'

He broke off. In the heat of the moment they had committed the cardinal sin of gathering in a group. Now, from both sides, he could hear crashing in the undergrowth as the gunmen closed in. Even as he roared a warning at Barret and McCrae he saw the big backwoodsman already moving. Then the two gunmen who had finished with Cotter and Strachan opened fire from deep cover.

Bullets snicked through leaves, sliced white wood from thin branches. One plucked at Hunter's hat. He spun, dropped to one knee and fired four fast shots into the woods. As he did so he heard the solid thud of a bullet hitting flesh. Out of the corner of his eye he saw Barret go down. McCrae ran to the fallen oilman, lay down his Sharps and bent over the still form. He looked across at Hunter and shook his head.

Dead – or OK? Hunter wondered.

Then he was concerned with his own safety. Another bullet screamed from the woods and smashed into the stock of his Winchester. The rifle fell from numbed hands, shattered at the pistol grip. Cursing, he kicked the useless weapon into the grass. Then, aware of McCrae standing spread-legged as he fired a volley of pistol bullets into the scrub, he drew his six-gun.

As he did so, another weapon joined in the fray. From the stack of equipment close to the derrick, muzzle flashes winked like blazing yellow eyes. One bullet thunked into a tree trunk close to Hunter. A second kicked up dirt between McCrae's feet, a third clipped the toe of his boot.

The backwoodsman jerked his head towards the danger. Hunter saw his lips tighten. Then, ignoring the steady, spaced shots coming from the woods, he dropped to his knee alongside Barret and picked up the Sharps.

He took his time. Hunter had dropped back to the edge of the woods. The gunmen raining fire down on them from the flanks had stopped shooting. The rifleman in cover beyond the derrick was strangely quiet.

'Step out,' McCrae said to Hunter. 'Show yourself.'

Do what? Hunter thought incredulously – and then he looked at the supremely confident McCrae and the powerful buffalo gun held rock steady in the trapper's capable hands and with a half smile he stepped out onto the trail.

At once the rifle in the drillings spat flame. The crack

was followed by a sickening thud. Hunter's big bay horse sighed and sank to its knees. Then the heavy Sharps boomed. Hunter saw the figure half sheltered by the stack of equipment blown backwards like a leaf caught in a gust of wind. As he went down his rifle fell, glittering in the pale moonlight.

From the woods, the two gunmen recommenced firing with their rifles.

Hunter was down close to the earth, looking sideways at McCrae.

'How's Barret?'

'Out – but alive.'

'My rifle's bust, my horse probably dead. You plugged that man out there on the drillings, that way's clear of danger. What say I carry Barret, you cover us and we make a run for the cabin?'

'Let's do it.'

Hunter holstered his pistol, bent over Barret. The man's eyes gleamed behind half-closed lids. Hunter scooped him up, threw him across his shoulders with a strangled grunt of effort. Blood was slick on his hands. Half-stooped, knees wobbling, he ran awkwardly with the dead weight. In that manner, soon gasping for breath, he made it down the slope and onto the rutted land around the drilling site.

Shots cracked, close behind him. McCrae was following, walking backward as he matched Hunter's speed. His steady shooting was forcing the men in the woods to keep their heads down. One shot did whine close overhead, and Hunter heard Barret give a low moan of fear.

Then he'd reached the cabin. He kicked the door. It swung open. He stepped inside, carefully lowered Barret to the floor close to one of the desks. He heard the door bang shut behind McCrae.

Despite the broken window, the oil lamp was still burning. By its glow Hunter saw McCrae walk away from the door and gaze carefully through the shattered glass.

'Whatever else we've done, we've got Barret back where he belongs,' Hunter said softly.

McCrae wasn't listening.

'That was Yantze under the derrick,' he said. 'He's dead. Flint. . . ? I couldn't tell.'

'Poor John,' Barret said hoarsely, and both men looked at him in amazement as he pushed himself up and sat with his back against the wall.

'One down, two to go,' Hunter said, and grinned at Barret.

McCrae was still at the window.

'If Yantze's out there, it must've been Jarrow out on one flank, Levin the other.'

'They're outside, we're inside,' Barret said. 'They've got to take the place all over again, just the two of them.'

'No,' McCrae said. 'Not two.' He glanced sideways at Hunter. 'Remember Quint, and the danger he posed. I hear horses, I think he's arrived. Not only that, I think it's likely he and Jarrow will come to an agreement. So it's not two, it's five. Which means this could be a long and bloody night.'

TWENTY-ONE

A long night didn't figure in Morgan Jarrow's plans. Five minutes was all the time the defenders trapped inside the cabin were allowed. Jarrow, it seemed, was still hoping to get a good night's sleep.

Away from the window at last, McCrae got Barret up and seated in one of the stuffed chairs beyond the enclosure of desks and out of the line of fire. There was a bloody wound in the fleshy part of the oilman's shoulder. Shock had knocked him out. A medical cabinet was fixed to one of the walls. McCrae dressed the wound, and pronounced him fit.

'Got the tools to do the job,' Hunter said, indicating the gun rack he'd noticed on his first visit.

'Could do with some more hands to hold 'em,' McCrae grumbled.

'Strachan, Cotter?' Hunter said. 'I sent them out there. What are their chances?'

'Dead,' McCrae said flatly. 'Both of them.'

And he was still standing with hands on hips, eyes bleak with memory, when the night exploded and a hail of bullets hammered into the walls of the cabin and came pouring in like hornets through the shattered window.

McCrae ran to the front wall, stood to one side of the window then risked a look out. The pistol he was carrying remained at his side. Bullets thudded into the logs. Muzzle flashes at the edge of the timber beyond the drillings were as bright as a summer storm.

'Key,' Hunter yelled.

Barret scrabbled at a drawer, tossed a jingling bunch to the marshal. Hunter unlocked the gun rack, took out a Winchester. Barret threw him a carton of shells. Hunter ran to the window, dropped down, thumbed bullets into the rifle's magazine.

'Methinks we're done for,' McCrae said, and Hunter looked at him in amazement.

'Call 'em army tactics, call 'em Indian tactics,' the trapper went on, 'I'd say Jarrow knows them all. He's got us pinned down. We go out the window or the door, we die—'

'There's no back entrance,' Barret blurted.

'—yeah, and I just saw Quint's boys, on foot, comin' out of the timber. I think they'll try to burn us out.'

As if to punctuate the trapper's words, the gunfire settled to a steady beat. Two men – probably Quint and Levin – were placing regular, well-aimed shots at window and door. Returning fire from the window was impossible. Leaving the cabin by either would have been suicide. As the minutes ticked by, McCrae reported on progress. Two men under the lofty derrick, messing with the oil, the equipment, the supplies. Now moving away to get around and behind the cabin. The flare of a match. Smoke and flame rising from a bundle of oil-soaked rags. Both of them gone now – out of sight.

And then the thump on the roof they'd all been waiting for: the slow crackle, increasing in intensity as the thin shingle roof caught fire; the almost instant glow overhead as the fire ate its way through; the stink of burning oil and shingle that quickly filled the air inside the room.

Barret had slumped down in the stuffed chair. His right arm was in a sling. His eyes appeared lifeless as he stared into space watching his dream go up in smoke.

Coughing, eyes watering, Hunter joined McCrae at the window. Just as he got there, Jarrow launched his attack. He used horses, leading a cavalry charge, followed by Quint and Levin. All three held their pistols high, yipping and hollering, coats flying, hat brims flattened by the wind. They split around the central derrick, then came together and bore down on the burning building. The only sound to be heard was the thunder of pounding hoofs, the crackle and hiss of the fire.

'Brace yourself,' McCrae said.

Barret had closed his eyes. Hunter was shaking his head in disbelief.

Then a shot rang out. Another. Someone was roaring an order.

'Jesus Christ on a donkey,' McCrae said, gazing out wide-eyed as he clutched excitedly at Hunter's shoulder.

Suddenly, the woods beyond the drillings were alive with men. They burst forth on an array of mounts, charged across the tract carrying every imaginable weapon. They advanced at a furious gallop, in line abreast, smashing through undergrowth, splashing through muddy pools lingering from the day's rain. In the wan moonlight they poured across the broken ground of the drillings in a surging wave, and in an instant Jarrow and Quint and Levin were engulfed, swallowed up, rendered insignificant.

Out of it all, as Hunter ran to the door and yanked it open to let in a blast of cold, fresh air, he saw one man mounted on a black horse looking towards the cabin.

Jake Rogers.

'The barber,' McCrae said. He was behind Hunter, supporting a groggy Barret. The oilman could not believe his eyes or his luck, and said so.

'It's not luck,' Hunter said. 'Rogers must've organized a citizen's army. I talked to him. He told me that whatever he did, it would be for the good of the town.'

'Now that he's here,' McCrae said, 'it occurs to me I could do with a shave.'

'Wrong,' Hunter said, and despite his crooked smile there was break in his voice. 'I reckon what you've been through, my friend, is the closest shave you're ever likely to get.'

McCrae grinned, and raised his eyes to heaven.

Yet as Hunter watched the big trapper help Barret out of the cabin and push through the crowd of horsemen towards where John Flint lay motionless beneath the derrick, he knew that if anyone over the past eventful days had been close to ruin, it was not McCrae. With a grimace he unpinned the marshal's badge from his

Confederate jacket, rubbed it on his sleeve, and sent it spinning high into the air.

It was over – whatever it was. And he had come out of it. Not rich. A little older. A lot wiser. And wasn't that as much as he could have expected?

Zac Hunter took a deep breath. Then he glanced once in the direction of Louisiana, and set about acquiring a horse for the long ride to the Sabine River, and the family home.

AUTHOR'S NOTE

It must be stressed that while the details of Edwin Drake's and Lyne Taliaferro Barret's drilling exploits in Pennsylvania and Texas are historically accurate, the events presented in this novel – including the gunfight on the Skillern tract – are figments of my imagination. Drake and Barret were real people, all others represented are fictional characters.

The facts

Edwin Drake struck oil in Pennsylvania in 1859, and his well produced up to twenty barrels a day (before burning down a few months after opening, and being swiftly replaced). From then on, the state's oil industry expanded rapidly: up to the East Texas oil boom of 1901, Pennsylvania was responsible for a half of the world's oil production.

Lyne Taliaferro Barret really did strike oil – on the Skillern tract in an area known as Oil Springs in Nacogdoches County – on 12 September 1866, at a depth of 106 feet. His well produced just ten barrels a day, and was unprofitable, but it proved that there was oil beneath the Texas soil.

Visitors can drive to the site of Texas' first oil well, but will find very little of interest. For years, former Nacogdoches Fire Chief Delbert Teutsch laboured to preserve the well area, and several others have tried in vain to get Texas Parks & Wildlife to develop a state historical park there.